OWL BE FUC'D

A FUC ACADEMY STORY

FIERCE FLEDGLINGS BOOK 6

MANDY ROSKO

1

TJ took the folder handed to him numbly, staring at the man across the desk.

The sudden urge to leap over it and strangle him put a light tremble in his hands.

"Am I dismissed?"

"No." Albert Huntly raised his index finger at him, pushing his giant glasses up his nose with his other finger. "Nothing permanent. You just need some time off after what happened."

Bullshit.

"Nolan and Diane both cleared me physically. I got a psych eval done."

Albert shook his head. "That's great, but you're taking at least the next two weeks off anyway."

The notice in TJ's hands crumpled as he clenched his fingers around it.

"But why? What the hell did I do?"

Albert's owl eyes flashed. His voice steeled to something cold and sharp, compared to its usual friendly warmth. "You're barely more than a cadet and you nearly burned alive in that facility *after* getting kidnapped. That's not something that goes away."

"I'm *fine*. I want to work! I need to work."

"This is *not* a punishment," Albert said, leveling him with the kind of stare only a bird of prey could give. "But you are taking it. It's paid leave. So go and relax. Just stay the hell away from here for a little while."

"Why?" TJ wasn't letting this go. It bothered him on a deeper level, which he couldn't explain.

Albert briefly closed his eyes, as if he was the one struggling for patience with all this. "Because you're poking your nose around in cases that don't involve you."

His defenses immediately rose up. "So, because I talked to Rachel twice I'm being put on leave?"

"Because you talked to her twice, and to her mate John Marsh three times, without letting us know." Albert leaned back in his chair. The way he crossed his arms made his biceps look surprisingly big.

Reminding TJ that he probably shouldn't pick fights with the guy who could fly and had claws.

"Did you think we wouldn't find out?"

TJ rolled his eyes.

"Are you a child? Answer the question."

TJ felt his spine go stiff. "To be honest, I thought you wouldn't."

Because he hadn't expected John to rat him out. The damn bitch.

Albert's nostrils flared, his lips thin. "You're not on that case, and they're both being taken care of."

"Fantastic."

"Don't get cute." Albert's eyes flashed. "You're lucky a paid leave is what you're given."

"I know," TJ said, clenching his teeth.

"What the hell were you thinking?"

It took everything he had to answer in a neutral voice, to relax his spine and hands, and just bend over and take it. "I shouldn't've gone, I know. You're right."

"But you did," Albert said. "You've also been doing a few other things you knew we wouldn't appreciate."

That clenching in his gut started up again. His palms grew sweaty.

"Did she complain?" he demanded to know. He hadn't done anything that would warrant a complaint.

He didn't think so, anyway.

"I didn't threaten her, or her boyfriend. I just wanted to talk to her."

It hadn't been much of a conversation, and he hadn't meant to surprise her by just showing up at her new place... but still...

He'd needed to talk to her. Only Rachel could give him the answers he'd needed.

"She didn't complain," Albert said quickly. "That's not the issue. I don't need your reasons or your excuses. Everyone's got them." He inhaled deeply. "I get that better than anyone, but you're still taking the time off."

"If I can't?"

Albert drilled his fingertips again and again into the desk. TJ got that tight, twisting feeling in his chest again.

"TJ, you'd barely graduated FUCN'A" —the Furry United Coalition Newbie Academy— "when this happened to you. I know some of the senior agents can, and have, pulled some stunts from time to time, but you are not one of those agents. You don't have the experience, the seniority, the *anything*. You're a rookie."

It was a struggle to not clench his hands into fists around the dismissal papers.

It was true, but it stung to hear it.

TJ didn't *feel* like a rookie. He felt like he'd spent the last three hundred years of his life getting experimented on, stabbed with needles, poisoned with all kinds of chemicals, and examined under a million different microscopes.

Then another four years of his life trapped in his own body. The team at FUC did everything they could to reverse what had been done to him, but it still felt like more of the same at times.

Endless experiments. Endless needles. Endless fucking pain and tears and blood.

The doctors at FUC at least cared enough to not jab him so hard with those needles. To smile. To assure him they were doing what they could, and they answered all his questions without any shady dodging.

To give him hope that they could fix what had been done to him.

That was why he'd wanted to join. To be on the team and get through training at the Academy.

To help other people who'd had their lives stolen from them, like he had.

"I've got more experience than most of your other agents, and I don't care what anyone has to say about it."

"I know," Albert said, heaving a sigh of his own, his voice becoming a touch softer again. "But you're still dismissed until further notice."

TJ stood there, stewing in his rage and helplessness.

He should walk out. Albert had dismissed him; that's what that meant.

The man leaned back in his seat. He stared at TJ, as if he could read everything going on in his mind.

"Unless there was something else you wanted to say?"

TJ's adrenaline kicked back in. "Like what?"

He got another one of those cold, calculated stares. Like there was something else. Something they'd known for a long time. "You *know* what."

TJ KILLED the engine of his car. He sat there, stared at the front door to his house, and wished he could kill something for real.

He smacked his fist against the wheel about a dozen times before he stopped, out of breath, his fist pulsing hot with pain. He was *fucking pissed.*

He'd barely graduated, and already he was getting disciplined. Having to go through this goddamn song and dance just to show he was...

Loyal?

He fucking hated himself worse now than when his face had been fucked up beyond measure.

It was fucking horseshit.

A soft light briefly flared up inside his truck. TJ closed his eyes and leaned back in his seat, covering the light over his forehead with his hand before the stupid thing could get worse.

Before long, needle-pointed teeth could show up next, or buggy black eyes the size of baseballs.

Inhale. Exhale. Serenity now. He had this. He wasn't going to lose control.

He wasn't going to turn back into *that.*

He was fine.

Until he opened his eyes and saw who was standing next to his front door, looking at him through the windshield.

TJ wasn't feeling so serene all of a sudden. He shoved his way out of the truck, marching to the door.

No. *No.* Why the fuck was he here now?

"What are you doing here?"

Matthew frowned. His eyebrows had come back since the last time TJ saw the man, but there was still some discoloration on his face from the gasoline burns.

"You okay?" Matthew asked, like TJ wasn't staring at him like he was going to punch him. "Did something happen?"

Yes. A lot, actually.

"Your sister is fine," TJ said. "I just... I got put on leave for talking to her, though."

The words felt like sand grating his throat.

"She's really all right?"

TJ nearly popped his teeth clenching his jaw, irritated that Rachel was all Matthew seemed to care about.

"Yeah, she's good. Rachel's been getting taken care of by FUC for all the cooperating she's been doing. Her and John both."

Matthew's dark eyes flashed at the mention of the snake shifter. The guy his sister, Rachel, was shacking up with after their fuckhead dad tried burning down the compound where they came from—with TJ and Matthew still inside.

Bobby had already been dead.

The poor bastard. TJ still felt kind of sorry for him. The guy was a mess. Getting stuck partway through a transformation, especially as a tarantula shifter, was rough. TJ still shuddered thinking of his clicking mandibles and the long, pointy hairs that poked out from his lips and cheeks.

Bobby had been a massive asshole, but he didn't deserve to die like that, and he didn't deserve to have his body scorched in hundreds of gallons of gasoline in a hole in the ground either.

"John is still with her?"

"Last I checked." TJ kicked the toe of his shoe into the dirt. His hands still itched to wrap around something.

He would settle for Matthew's neck right around now.

He should tell him to leave. He would be doing the guy a favor.

"I'm sorry."

"Yeah, I know." TJ looked around. No one could see them. The house was pretty far out of the way, but there were still a few neighbours within sight of the place he was renting.

He *needed* to tell Matthew to go. Instead, he asked, "You wanna come inside?"

Matthew's huge shoulders sagged. The man could give Jack Reacher a run for his money, but he still looked dirty and tired. "Yeah, thanks."

TJ nodded.

This was so fucking stupid. What he was doing now would make what he'd done with Rachel and John look like a cake walk. Forget being forced to take time off. He'd get his shiny, brand-new FUC license entirely revoked for disobeying orders.

Matthew was a wanted man.

The guys back at the office seemed to think Matthew knew where his daddy had gone. TJ was inclined to believe he didn't but only because Matthew was the one with the burn scars still healing all over him.

After he'd dragged TJ out of that compound before it completely went up in flames.

TJ unlocked the door. He felt Matthew's hulking presence as he opened it up and stepped inside. The guy was broader and taller than TJ was.

He flipped the light on, kicked off his shoes, and immediately headed for the kitchen. "You wanna drink?"

"A beer if you got it."

"I don't." TJ opened the fridge, ignoring the last three beer bottles he had sitting on the bottom shelf, grabbing a soda can instead. "This is what I got." He tossed it to Matthew, who easily caught it, cracking it open with a hiss. He tilted his head back and drank damn near the whole can, his scarred Adam's apple working with each swallow before he finally stopped with a heavy sigh.

"Thanks." He pressed the rest of the can to the side of his face, which still had some burns. They wrapped around the side of his face, trailing from his ear to his square jaw and down his neck. Looking at him from one side, it would be hard to tell they were even there, but from this side, it was like a grotesque tongue licking his face.

TJ winced at the crude thought.

Wasn't so long ago that his face looked much worse.

"Does it hurt?"

"What?" Matthew briefly sounded confused before understanding flickered across his face. "Oh, no," he said quickly, pulling the can away. "I was just hot. Don't worry."

"I wasn't worried." TJ ran his tongue over his teeth, looking away. "You can wash your clothes and have a shower if you want. Where are you staying now?"

He should say something about the conversation with Albert. He needed to warn him.

"Found another little fishing cabin yesterday. There's no running water, though, but the lake is nice."

"That's not going to work forever," TJ said, hating himself and saying nothing about what Albert wanted. He reminded himself that he was pissed off at Matthew and he didn't owe him anything else.

TJ took one of the beers and made a show of twisting the cap off right in front of Matthew before having a long, satisfying drink. Matthew looked at the beer, then at him, a bit of a bitch face coming along, but he didn't comment.

He felt like an asshole. "This one was mine. I had dibs."

That seemed to satisfy Matthew. "Well, it's your house, thank you for having me at all."

He said it a little stiffly, but TJ still felt like a jerk.

This was a shit ton of trouble right now, but Matthew saved his life. Letting him shower and eat at his place was the least he could do.

Not Matthew's fault TJ felt guilty and angry so much of everything because Albert wanted...

TJ leaned against the doorway to the kitchen, banishing thoughts about what happened earlier with the owl shifter.

For now.

It was too late to do anything anyway.

"You just come here to ask about Rachel?" he asked. Was he possibly hoping for something different?

"She's my sister." Matthew's thumb trailed across the sweat of his can. "I need to take care of her."

TJ nodded, disappointed.

He shouldn't be.

TJ didn't have anything of a social life to speak of, and Matthew was, at this point, the only thing close to a friend he had.

Which was pathetic on several different scales. Matthew only came here for the food, hot water, and news of his sister, not because he wanted any of TJ's company.

"Yeah. She's not telling them anything about you, as far as I'm aware. Sticking to her story about not being able to remember her life before the bunker."

"It's not a story," Matthew said.

"I know." TJ took another long swig from his bottle. "Apparently, getting experimented on and changed into something a little more than human messes with memories. You two aren't the only ones who don't remember your lives before getting stuck in that place."

The staff at FUCN'A had become experts at working with rescued experiments in that kind of situation. Albert and the agents of FUC could help Matthew. He didn't have to run.

TJ had told Matthew this a dozen or more times, but he didn't want to hear it. He didn't want to trust them.

Soon he wouldn't have a choice.

Matthew was silent for a long moment. His lips pressed in a fine line as he gripped his Coke can a little too hard. He seemed to be looking at something far away.

"He wasn't your dad."

Matthew shook his head. "You don't know that for sure."

"I'm willing to bet everything in my bank account on it." Which wasn't much, but it meant something to say it.

"You might have a family out there. People who miss you."

Matthew's jaw clenched. He looked away from TJ, drank from his can, and said nothing.

They'd had this talk before. Matthew just wasn't willing to hear it.

TJ tried again. One more time.

"The doctors they have at FUC are the best. They already did a blood test on Rachel. If you would let them do one to you—"

"No."

TJ snapped his mouth shut. The word, snarled so fiercely, sent a shiver through his spine.

Matthew stared at him like he was the enemy.

TJ felt a little like the enemy. He understood Matthew's distrust. Bad enough knowing the man he thought of as his father had abandoned him, but that the guy had lit up the only home Matthew knew and left it to burn...

TJ still wasn't sure if the psycho doctor knew Matthew would be in there. He hoped to God for Matthew's sake that he hadn't.

He had to tread lightly, but he wasn't backing down. This was his house, dammit. "FUC is still working on putting together anything that could've survived the compound fire. Trying to repair it and read the data. They have a habit of figuring things out eventually. Getting a blood test and finding out where you came from would help you."

"I can't go in."

"If you would just cooperate—"

"I said no."

Matthew's eyes flashed red. TJ's spine went stiff, the hairs on his arms standing straight.

He knew this feeling. The scared, can't move because there was a threat in front of him sort of feeling.

He didn't like it, especially in his own house.

Not like he was about to back down, even if they both knew Matthew could take him in a fight.

"Put the claws away or get out."

Matthew blinked, frowned, and looked down at his hands. Hooked talons were in the place where his finger-nails should be.

They melted away quickly.

TJ hated to admit it, but he was relieved.

"I wouldn't've—"

"Don't care. *Don't* do it again." TJ glanced down at his bottle and rolled his eyes before turning his back, returning to the fridge, and yanking out a fresh one.

It hissed as he uncapped it. He needed a damn drink.

Mathew was suddenly right behind him. TJ felt his presence so easily these days.

"Aren't you trained to not turn your back on a potential threat?"

Fuck.

TJ slowly spun, dangling the neck of the beer in his fingers. "Are you a threat?"

He felt a little threatened but not in the normal way. He couldn't describe it, but Matthew, standing so close, sent a different sort of chill through his body.

Anticipation.

"No, but you're a bad actor." Matthew reached passed him to the nearly empty bottle TJ had put on the counter. There was a single mouthful left. "And an asshole." He eyed the second bottle in TJ's hand. "And a liar."

Matthew said it with just enough of a smile that TJ didn't hold the insult against him. Matthew took the last small drink from the bottle.

"Whatever. You're a fugitive. I'm not getting you drunk in my house."

Matthew rolled his eyes.

"I'm serious. You can't hold your booze, man."

"It's not that bad," he muttered.

Matthew really couldn't remember what happened the last time, could he?

Probably for the best.

"Uh-huh." Now TJ felt better. He felt more like he was talking to an old friend, not some guy he barely knew, who, for some reason, TJ had let hide away from the agents of FUC so Matthew could slink around town, doing God only knew what.

TJ owed the man his life. That wasn't just it, though.

He was so fucking stupid.

And an asshole.

Matthew was right.

"Go take a shower. I'm gonna order a pizza. You want anything on it?"

Have to keep Matthew around for a little while longer. If he's here, it will be easier. Easier than Albert and a team surrounding some shitty little fishing cabin with weapons and a fight breaking out. TJ could help him here.

"I can't pay you back," Matthew said. He always said it.

"It's on me. Get out of here," TJ said, reaching for his phone. "You smell like fish."

Matthew stood there, not moving for a minute.

It had TJ's hackles rising. "What?"

Matthew wet his lips. He wouldn't look at TJ. He got weird when he did that. "Nothing. Thank you. For the meal and... everything else."

TJ's breath inexplicably caught. Guilt. Raw, acidic, burning, and hissing guilt spread like poison in his chest.

"Whatever. You'd starve if I didn't feed you. You need to get better at hunting."

"Says the lightbulb fish," Matthew said, rolling his eyes and wandering off. He already knew where the bathroom was. TJ had long since stopped locking the door to his bedroom, not too worried that Matthew would go snooping, but all his devices were still password protected, so it wasn't as if he was being entirely reckless.

Matthew had been here probably a dozen times since the fire. He'd slept over three or four of those times as well. TJ had gotten used to him being around.

Stupid to have thought FUC wouldn't have noticed.

Before he could dial for that pizza, Rachel's name popped up with a text. TJ blinked, almost not believing his eyes.

It was the first time she'd ever directly reached out to him. He'd always contacted her.

And it couldn't have been on a worse night.

Hi, it's Rachel. I'm sorry. Have you heard from Matt lately?

What the fuck? The whole goddamn world was out to make him feel like a piece of shit today it seemed.

Especially when the next text came in.

There was no name, but TJ knew it was from the team at FUC Albert had set up.

We're in position. Stay clear.

2

Matthew stood under the shower spray, staring at the grime that slid down his body and oozed down the drain. He clenched his hands again and again. He wanted to punch something, but he was in TJ's house.

Wouldn't do to break anything when he was a barely welcome guest here.

No wonder the guy had cringed at him. It had been a long time since he'd properly showered. Since he'd properly eaten, too.

He let his talons out, having a look at them. Despite his best efforts, he hadn't caught much for eating.

No wonder his father wasn't making contact. He was a fucking failure.

Matthew blew out a breath, reached for TJ's liquid Irish Spring, and started to properly scrub down.

Maybe it was for the best that his sister was with that damned snake. John was the absolute last person in the world Matthew wanted Rachel involved with, but with him, she could have three meals a day, a warm bed to sleep in, clothes that weren't filthy, and maybe a chance at a normal life.

Whatever that looked like for people like them.

Not wanting to use up too much of TJ's hot water, Matthew quickly rinsed and stepped out of the shower. He heard the brief sound of voices outside and tensed.

A threat.

No. He relaxed, the squeezing around his heart easing off as the words formed and took shape through the doors.

"Keep the change. Have a good one."

"Thanks, pal, any time."

Pizza was here. TJ had paid. Of course he did. He always did. Not like Matthew had anything to offer him.

The door shut, and the delivery guy left.

Matthew took a breath, hands clenching around the bathroom countertop.

TJ wasn't turning him in. For whatever reason, the guy had yet to call FUC whenever Matthew showed up at his doorstep. Matthew wasn't entirely sure why that was. It certainly wasn't because TJ had some friendly feelings toward Matthew. Ever since TJ had left him alone the first time, to recover from his burns. the guy had been pissed.

Understandable. Matthew had admitted he was planning on turning TJ over to his father.

Not your father, a nasty little voice inside his head hissed.

Bazyli Smith, that goddamn bastard, was not his father.

Yet Matthew had nearly handed TJ over to him.

Another experiment. Another chance to make things better for Rachel.

So he'd thought.

After the fire, after TJ had taken the time to bandage his burns, Matthew had felt probably a little abandoned, and shocked, hoping his father hadn't lit the place up on purpose with him inside.

He'd saved TJ's life, but the man had also saved his, and had cared enough to not abandon him in the woods and leave him with his burns, so Matthew had admitted to him what he'd planned on doing.

TJ had sneered at him, didn't say a single word, and walked out.

He'd been right to do that.

Earlier, TJ had promised to turn him over to FUC within twenty-four hours.

And then the guy just... never did.

TJ never told them about him. Never told Matthew's sister about the red water tanks. Never let on to the fox shifter that Bazyli was likely not her father, either. That Matthew was not her brother.

Matthew couldn't figure it out. Same as he couldn't entirely figure out why he kept coming back.

Because you have nowhere else to go, idiot.

Yeah, *sure*, and because TJ was the one feeding him, yes. TJ also had a working computer he let Matthew use, and was Matthew's only chance of getting any information on Rachel.

The agents of the Furry United Coalition weren't stupid. They watched Rachel like hawks. From what Matthew understood, they barely tolerated John, the snake shifter who'd betrayed them.

Who Rachel loved, for some reason Matthew couldn't fathom.

But John was no longer the guy FUC wanted to throw into a cage now that he was cooperating with them, giving them whatever info they wanted.

Still, the one time Matthew had tried to get close to Rachel's house, it nearly landed him in a cage.

His owl shape was too big. It wasn't exactly easy to stealthily swoop in, hide in the trees, and wait for the coast to be clear when he was the size of a small bear and had long, pointed saber-teeth that stretched down from his beak and nearly touched his talons.

Brute strength he could do—TJ was right to be worried about that—but stealth and hiding? No. Not his thing.

A soft knock sounded at the door. "Hey, Matt, pizza's here."

Matthew jumped. Then he cleared his throat, his knuckles white from gripping the bathroom counter. "I'll be right there. Thank you."

A brief pause outside. "I took your clothes and put them in the wash. I got something else for you in the meantime, though. It's sitting on the floor outside the door."

Really?

"And Rachel just texted me."

Matthew's breath caught.

"She's asking about you. I didn't reply yet. Don't want to give FUC anything to track."

Matthew's heart slammed. He hadn't spoken a word to Rachel since they'd left the compound. Since everything had gone to shit. Not even over the phone or text.

But TJ's last statement gave Matthew pause. He didn't often comment on FUC activities, and if he was worried about being tracked now, then they must be breathing down his neck about his involvement at the compound.

"Th-thank you," he said, the words catching in his throat.

He sensed TJ stepping away from the door. Matthew waited a minute but then got curious. TJ had prepared clothes for him?

He opened the door, half expecting to see something designed to humiliate him. A clown costume. A giant pink onesie. That seemed like the sort of thing TJ would do.

But, no. The clothes were normal. They'd been worn before. Through the scent of clean detergent, Matthew could make out the scents of many people. Faint, but it was there.

Used clothes, but they were still good. Clean, no holes, all the buttons in place, and the laces on the boots seemed to be strong enough.

Something tightened in the back of Matthew's throat. He heard the gentle clank of dishes and cups in the kitchen.

"Thank you, TJ," he said, just loud enough that TJ could hear it.

TJ liked to punish Matthew from time to time, but as it was, he was also the most generous person Matthew had come across out in the real world.

"Don't mention it." TJ's voice sounded tired. "Get dressed and come eat." A brief hesitation. "You can... spend the night if you want."

Another fluttering in Matthew's chest. Something hopeful rising. He didn't spend the night often. The last time he had...

He closed his eyes. The memory of TJ's surprisingly soft mouth...

Yeah, now he remembered why TJ got prickly from time to time.

Matthew got dressed. The layers were nice, the jeans a touch too big, but that made them comfortable. The white T-shirt sat nicely under the blue plaid, and the clean socks in the tan boots almost made him feel normal.

He didn't have a good frame of reference for what normal could be, but this had to be it, and once again,

Matthew found himself overflowing with that sense of gratitude.

Careful. He had to be so careful. The last time he'd been this grateful he'd done something that had TJ throwing him out of the house.

He always seemed to be doing things that made the guy want to leave or push him away.

Matthew stepped into the kitchen. It was separated from the living room couch and TV by a small kitchen island. TJ was putting slices onto plates, and for the life of him, Matthew couldn't figure out why the man insisted on sharing everything equally.

Especially since Matthew had nothing to pay the man back with.

His stomach constricted painfully.

TJ looked up. He was a shifter too, even if he was some strange breed of fish. Of course he'd heard Matthew's stomach rumbling.

"You wanna beer?"

Matthew almost smiled. "I thought you were out?"

TJ half shrugged. Now he was the one who wouldn't look Matthew in the eyes. "I think you're fine if you have one. Just the one."

"I'll be thankful for whatever you decide to give."

"Yeah, yeah." TJ yanked open the fridge and pulled out the bottle, holding it out for Matthew to take.

Matthew reached for it.

Their fingers touched.

He paused.

TJ paused.

They stared at each other briefly before TJ was the one to break. He cleared his throat, pulling his hand away and taking two steps back.

Just enough to look natural without making it seem as though he were retreating.

"Here's your plate."

"Thank you." Matthew's stomach rumbled again. The scent in the air was already delicious. Meat and sauce and melting mozzarella cheese made his mouth water.

TJ's throat worked with a hard swallow as he stuffed a slice into his mouth, taking a big bite.

Somehow that was all it took for Matthew to lick his lips.

He shook it off, standing on his end of the island, letting TJ have his space.

"When's the last time you ate?" TJ asked suddenly.

"Not that long ago."

Three of the longest days of his life.

Matthew knew he was losing weight. He wasn't the best hunter in the world. He was learning, but the days between catches were brutal. The longest days were when he couldn't catch anything and when he was too proud to go crawling to TJ for food.

Every instance where TJ fed him always felt a little warmer. As if the man was binding Matthew to him more and more with every meal.

It took everything he had to not moan around the food in his mouth. He wanted so badly to stuff his face and even take what TJ had.

For all the faults of Bazyli Smith, the man who claimed to be his father, he'd always fed him.

Before he tried to burn him alive.

TJ stared at him. "Right, okay. You wanna come and sit down? I haven't thought about what I was going to send to Rachel."

Oh, right, his sister.

Matthew was grateful for the invitation to actually sit

and eat like a human, not some animal. And he was too eager to keep shoveling food into his face and hear more about what was happening with Rachel to hesitate as he followed TJ to the couch.

"How is she? Is the snake treating her well?" He stuffed another bite into his mouth.

"She didn't write anything but what I told you." TJ pulled out his phone and actually held it out for Matthew to see for himself.

"I wasn't accusing you of lying."

TJ yanked his hand back, looking away. He looked mortified. "I-I know, but I still wanted you to see it."

Matthew nodded, guilt burning in his stomach like acid. TJ was doing so much for him already. He didn't mean to make him uncomfortable. It was enough of a risk for a rookie agent reaching out to a witness on a case he wasn't involved in. Matthew wasn't educated in many things, but he knew that much.

TJ even tried to keep communication between himself and Rachel in person. No messages. Nothing that any agent of FUC could read after the fact or trace.

"If she's texting you, it's because there's a problem." The pizza sat heavily in his gut. "Could she be in danger? Would FUC tell you about that?"

"She's fine," TJ said quickly. "No, don't worry. I'm sure of it. Even if they didn't tell me anything, she would."

"But FUC still does not wish for you to have contact with her?"

"Either that, or John doesn't."

Matthew clenched his teeth. "If the stupid bastard knows what's good for him, he would keep your talks to himself."

TJ shrugged, staring at the TV, which was turned off. "It might not've been him. These people are good at what they do. There's only so long anyone can keep a secret from them." TJ played with one of his crusts. "Albert said there wasn't a complaint, and I guess I believe him, but if they don't want me making contact, then there's not much I can do."

And they didn't want TJ making contact because he was, technically, also a victim of that same compound. Bazyli, that dirty fox shifter, had abandoned the compound, the only home Matthew had ever known, and had activated what was essentially a kill switch for the entire damn place. The barrels and barrels of fuel, which Matthew was told were used for the backup generators, suddenly released through the sprinkler systems.

Matthew still shuddered, thinking of the smell as they were soaked. He'd looked at TJ, and the terror in his eyes, as they both realized what was coming.

If they hadn't already been so close to the surface and the stream of water that ran through the compound's pipes…

TJ would be dead, and Matthew wouldn't ever forgive himself.

Matthew's scars licked across his throat, the side of his face, and down his left shoulder and arm, a constant reminder.

Some days he felt he deserved them more than others.

TJ had made it out with minimal burning. The only scar left that Matthew could see was a bit of red over his right hand. That burn snaked up his arm and touched his ribs. Matthew had seen it during one of his visits, briefly, when TJ had left the bathroom after a shower and walked quickly to his room with a towel around his waist.

Matthew couldn't stop staring.

At his scar.

He was healing better than Matthew was. Which was good. Matthew could hardly see the discoloration on his hand at all anymore. Still, it was there. Because of him.

TJ could not be on a case in which he'd been a victim.

And he could not speak to Rachel, because the FUC agents were concerned that he was in contact with someone from the inside.

Which he was. FUC could be spying on them right now for all either of them knew.

"Does Rachel seem happy? When you speak to her?"

TJ stared ahead, bringing his paper cup of soda to his mouth. "She's doing well. She misses you. She worries."

Matthew didn't want her worried.

But part of him liked knowing he had someone who worried about him at all. Someone in the world who cared, when so few people did.

TJ seemed to care a little. For whatever reason. He was glad for that.

"Does she... suspect anything? With the tanks?"

TJ paused mid-chew, the pizza feeling like a lump that was suddenly hard to swallow. Matt referred to the tanks they'd seen before the fire destroyed them. Tanks with pink fluid, faded labels, and failed experiments. Some so old they were rotting in their fluids.

Proof that Matthew and Rachel were not their father's children. They were just a few more miserable, kidnapped orphans of experimentation.

"*No*." TJ looked him right in the eye, his voice firm. "I never... I don't think anyone even... No."

Fuck, TJ wanted to say more, wanted to give details, but

he couldn't because he didn't know who was listening in now.

If Matthew picked up on his nerves, he didn't mention it. He seemed satisfied by TJ's answers.

Yes, it was difficult to keep secrets from the agents of FUC. He'd been stupid to think he ever could.

Matthew sat a little straighter, the energy around him sizzling like a sudden live wire. "Come with me."

TJ looked at him. His voice came out in a small, embarrassing squeak. "What?"

Matthew's eyes were bright. "You want to find my father, to get back at him for what he did to you, correct?"

"And to Bobby," TJ said. He'd never liked the guy, but he wasn't okay with what happened to him either.

Matthew inched closer. He lifted his hand, like he wanted to touch TJ's shoulder.

He dropped his hand instead. "Then come with me. You said it was difficult to keep secrets from these FUC people. It's just a matter of time before they find out about this and I'm in a cage."

"They won't..." TJ rubbed his eyes. "They won't go that far. They won't cage you."

Albert had promised him that.

Matthew snorted. "You don't know that."

"I do know that. If you would just..." *Listen.*

But there was nothing to listen to. It was too late.

TJ knew that the instant there was a sharp knock at the door.

Dread filled him like an icy sludge.

Had the agents outside gotten sick of standing back and waiting for Matthew to spill all the juicy details they wanted?

Matthew sat ramrod stiff. "Did you order something else?"

TJ was supposed to say yes. He was supposed to make Matthew feel at ease so he wouldn't run.

He couldn't.

TJ just fucking couldn't. A horrible guilt got to him before anything else could be said.

He couldn't look Matthew in the eye. His heart pounded. And like a fucking coward, he hid his face in his hands.

Matthew jumped up, stood over him.

TJ sat where he was. He was such a fucking pussy. He couldn't even look the guy in the face. He wished Matthew would punch him and get it over with.

"You—"

The front door burst open.

Sounded like the agents damn near took it off its hinges.

Matthew ran, bolting in the other direction as FUC agents filled TJ's house.

TJ couldn't look. He cringed at the shouting, the sound of broken glass, and felt like absolute shit.

3

Matthew pulled at the chains around his wrists. Bolted down to a metal table in a simple concrete room, the chair he sat in was also bolted into the floor so he couldn't break it apart and use it as a possible weapon.

He was fucking stewing.

He should have seen it coming. If he was honest, this was a little bit his own fault.

TJ had finally done it. He'd finally turned him in.

Fucking asshole.

He said he hadn't responded to Rachel's text because he didn't want to give FUC anything to track. Had Rachel even messaged him? Or was that bullshit too?

Matthew pulled again on the chain, checking for the thousandth time if there was any give to the bolt.

There wasn't.

Someone was definitely watching him through that two-way mirror. He wished he could see who it was. If it was TJ, he wasn't sure how he would react.

He was furious at being captured, still, he couldn't be too mad at the guy. TJ was a saint for putting up with him for as long as he had, and Matthew couldn't expect him to keep harboring a fugitive forever. Not when his job was at stake.

The door opened.

Matthew almost stood on habit. His father had demanded Matthew stand whenever he walked into a room.

But this wasn't his dad, and he was still chained down. Matthew clenched his hands instead, observing the two men who walked in.

He had no idea who they were. They looked a little alike, he supposed. Probably brothers. Partners about to question the dangerous shifter from the hole in the ground where Rachel had lived and where that snake, John, had been held against his will.

The men sat, dropping some yellow folders onto the table.

"You want a coffee?" asked the taller of the two men. "Something to eat?"

Matthew said nothing.

Speaking casually, offering food and drinks was supposed to be a method for lowering his guard. Making him believe these were his friends and his allies. People who would assist him instead of throwing him away when they got what they wanted.

Matthew didn't know much, but his father—*not my father*—had taught him that much.

The taller male sighed.

Matthew thought smelled a little like a cat. They both did, though the taller man seemed more... wild. Like he was a lion or a panther, something meant to be a threat. The shorter of the two gave Matthew the impression of a house cat. Something smaller that could blend in and walk out and about and people would not bat an eye at the sight of him.

Matthew envied that. He could never fly or hunt where there were people close. Not without the locals bringing out their guns or calling the tabloids.

Both men had black hair. Both were lean, and both were wearing the sort of suit that told Matthew he was in a lot of shit.

The taller of the two had a striped blue tie. The shorter had a red tie.

Red Tie cleared his throat. "I'm Agent Tybalt, and this is my brother, Agent Tybalt."

"You can call me Sam," Red Tie said. "This is Steve."

"Do you know why you're here?" Steve asked.

Because TJ finally got sick of his shit and turned him in. How long had he been thinking about doing that?

Since the night they got drunk together, most likely.

Christ.

Steve sighed. He opened one of the folders. Inside, the first thing was a photo of Rachel.

Fury spread through him. It was one thing to keep him locked up, and another to throw his sister in his face. Matthew tried to stand, immediately pulling against the chains that held him, and against the table that was bolted to the floor.

Neither agent moved. They remained perfectly calm, as if he hadn't looked ready to attack. Sam briefly glanced to the mirror, though. He barely turned his head, but Matthew caught it.

Right. There were probably a dozen or so men behind that glass ready to come in here and kick his ass if he so much as looked at them the wrong way.

Fuck. He took a deep breath and settled back in his chair. "What do you want?"

"You ready to talk?" Sam asked.

"If you even think about hurting my sister," Matthew hissed, "I'll fucking kill you."

The men looked at each other. Steve gave a tired shrug.

"We're not going to hurt her. We're not Mastermind, or Mother, or your father, or any of the half-dozen people who got it in their heads that they can kidnap and experiment on people," Sam said, flipping to another photograph.

A grotesque face. Hideous. Matthew winced at the sight of it.

Large, bulbous eyes, teeth so long they stretched out the jaw of the poor man to the point that they were clearly causing him pain and discomfort. That wasn't even taking into account the needle-like look of them.

They were like porcupine quills. They were long and curved, some of them puncturing into the swollen lips, creating infection, blood, and pus. The guy looked miserable. Like he wanted to cry or end his life or vanish into a pit and never be seen ever again.

"Do you know who this is?" Steve asked, spinning the photo around and pushing it toward Matthew.

Matthew leaned away from it, as if the thing was going to infect him and make him look just like that.

"Know him?"

Both agents stared at him expectantly. Neither said anything further. As patient as ever.

Matthew looked again, and in an instant, it clicked. "That's TJ?" he asked, though he wasn't really wondering.

TJ had said he'd been messed up, that the experiments done on him had left him in a state like Bobby. Stuck somewhere in the middle between human and animal—fish, in TJ's case. Forced to carry around some of the features of his animal on his face because he couldn't fully shift. Couldn't shift at all. Could only *be* the hybrid creature.

TJ had talked about his teeth, about the horror of it, the pain, but Matthew hadn't thought... it never occurred to him that it could be...

This was fucking terrible. Matthew pulled the photo closer.

Jesus, TJ looked so... normal now. Matthew had listened to how TJ had described himself, and he knew the man felt like shit for it, but Matthew had always assumed he might have looked a little like Bobby.

Bobby had been bad. The tarantula hairs and mandibles were horrible to look at, but Matthew had gotten used to them quickly. He could eventually look at Bobby without cringing.

This...

"Why are you showing me this?"

"To show you what we try to do for the people we take in. We're trying to stop the experiments," Sam said. He pushed a few more photos Matthew's way. Before and after photos, Matthew assumed.

A woman with scales on her face and arms and then they were gone. A man with colorful feathers protruding from his neck and cheeks, giant red swells, like oversized pimples, where the feathers grew blemishing his skin, and then a photo of him looking happy and smiling with what Matthew assumed was his family.

"We're not the bad guys," Steve said, standing and leaning over the table.

Matthew tensed, until Steve produced a key and unlocked the handcuffs. "You don't have to be scared of us."

The chains fell off his wrists with a heavy, metallic clank.

"I was never scared of you," Matthew said, kind of annoyed they thought so.

"You hid from us like you were," Sam said. "You got TJ caught up in your nonsense, too."

"Where is he?" Matthew wanted to see TJ for himself. "Everything that happened was on me. I threatened him. You don't have to fire him."

"He'd be fired if you *had* threatened him." Sam fixed Matthew with a steely gaze. "We need agents we can trust who won't be manipulated by others or, at the very least, can find ways of letting us know what's going on if they're in trouble."

Matthew felt his talons coming out. Would the man's neck be soft and warm if he pushed them into the skin?

"He's not getting fired," Steve clarified. "He told us everything. You saved his life. Definitely saved him from some pretty bad burn scars." He eyed the side of Matthew's face. "He wanted to help you and was trying to convince you to come in."

"So why isn't he here?"

"Because we found out about you before he told us." Sam pulled the photos together, tapping them on the table. "We've suspected for a while. We've actually been watching his place, and you, for a few weeks."

Matthew clenched his teeth. "It really is difficult to keep secrets from you people."

Steve grinned like Matthew had just said something funny. Sam crossed his arms.

"TJ is being removed, temporarily, from active duty. For his failure to not bring you to our attention sooner. He's going to be paid for the time off, so you don't have to worry."

"I'm not worried." A lie. He did worry for TJ, and what the guy would do if he didn't have a job or a way to pay his bills. At least Matthew hadn't completely ruined everything for him. "What do you want from me?"

Steve glanced more openly toward the mirror. Could he see the people standing behind it? Were they sending him signals even right now?

"We've spoken to your sister at least three dozen or more times already. She doesn't know where your father went. We believe her."

"She's a good person."

Sam finally smiled. Soft and barely there. "You want to look out for your sibling?"

"Of course I do," Matthew growled, realizing the trap he'd been caught in.

These two agents were brothers. They knew they could manipulate him with sibling love. They knew what they would do for each other, so they probably came in to test what Matthew would do for Rachel and use that against him.

"She answered our questions, provided blood tests, told us the layout of the bunker that was burned, and even a few things about you."

That got him like a stab in the heart.

"Don't worry. Nothing much," Steve said. "Mainly your favorite foods. How you were attacked and woke up with no memories. She spoke about teaching you to read. Little things."

He would still rather they didn't know any of that.

"She was trying to protect you. If you were involved in any of the kidnappings, she didn't tell us."

"I wasn't."

"Except for TJ."

Matthew clenched his teeth. "That wasn't the same."

"You weren't directly involved, but you were still involved. It doesn't matter how much or how little."

"Will you please get to the point?"

"Fine," Sam said. "Cooperate with us and we'll find out where you really came from. Any jail sentence you receive will be minimized and FUC will continue to look out for your sister financially until she and John can take care of themselves. Considering where she came from, she won't exactly be easily employed."

Mother fuckers.

"And TJ keeps his job? You won't hold that against him either?"

The men looked at each other.

Matthew decided to explain before they could glance at the window again. "I pulled him away from the bunker before he could burn, but he took care of me when I was wounded. He fed me and didn't turn me into you fucks the instant he could."

"Is that everything?"

Matthew felt his face get shockingly hot. Anything else was not their damn business.

But, wait... Like a shot of lightning, a brilliant idea suddenly hit him.

"If I do anything to help you people, I want TJ there. He needs to be part of it."

Both agents frowned.

Matthew was certain he heard a muffled banging noise beyond the two-way mirror.

"Why?" Sam asked. "Aren't you mad at him?"

"I am, but I still trust him infinitely more than any of you. I want him part of the team. And I want to see my sister. Whenever I want. I want to speak with her myself and know she's all right."

He had no basis to make these demands. He knew that

Matthew waited, his breath held, for them to decide.

4

The house was small, quaint and out of the way. More of a cottage than a house. TJ had been there a few times, but this was the first time with other FUC agents—and Matthew.

Rachel had been told they were coming, and she flew out the door when her brother approached.

"Matthew!"

The delighted shriek of the red-haired woman was almost a shock. Much different than the shy and cautious woman TJ had gotten to know.

She threw herself into her brother's arms, and TJ got a nice, melty feeling in his gut. The grin on Matthew's face was heartwarming, too, as he hugged his sister tight, for what was probably the first time since they'd left their father's compound. It shot something painful into TJ's chest.

He shouldn't be here for this, intruding on such a beautiful, private moment.

Matthew held her tight and actually did a little spin before planting her feet back down. He didn't let her go, even though he had to bend over to hang on, his large hands gripping her shoulders. Matthew asked her some questions, his voice low. TJ couldn't make out what was said, but he didn't want to hear it either.

Matthew was pretty tall. He towered over his sister. They looked nothing alike at all, despite, supposedly, being siblings.

They likely weren't.

An image of the tanks flashed in TJ's mind. Would Matthew eventually tell her about them? He said he would, when she was ready. TJ sure as hell hadn't mentioned them to anyone.

Subject Number Thirteen: Rachel.

TJ hadn't had enough time to figure out exactly what was going on there, but it seemed undeniable that Bazyli had been growing humans. Clones, it seemed.

God. TJ didn't know this woman very well, but he couldn't imagine what learning about the tanks would do to her. Didn't want that heartbreak for her.

Steve, who was there to watch over both TJ and Matthew, stood next to TJ like nothing was out of the ordinary, like he was used to watching personal, happy family reunions and it just being business as usual.

"I thought you'd never come! I'm so happy!" Rachel exclaimed when they finally broke their hug.

"Of course I'd come to see you," Matthew said. "TJ has been giving you my messages?"

TJ cringed, knowing what the question really was. Matthew was double-checking that TJ hadn't lied to him about that too.

"Yes, but it wasn't nearly good enough. This is better."

Steve glanced at him. TJ didn't look back. Yes, he'd been caught talking to Rachel and harboring Matthew, but this was what FUC needed to confirm TJ had been working with

Matthew. Delivering messages between a witness and a fugitive.

Too bad TJ didn't feel bad about what he'd done. He didn't regret keeping Matthew's whereabouts secret. Not entirely.

But now that he could see how happy Matthew was to hold his sister, to grab her by the shoulders and make sure, with his own eyes, that she was all right, TJ realized he should have done more to convince the guy to turn himself in.

Matthew would have had this sooner.

"I'm so happy you're here!" Rachel said, so excited that her cute little red panda ears started to form where her real ones were. Her nose got a little more pointy. Whiskers started to emerge.

Matthew smiled like he'd seen this a thousand times before, scrubbing his hand through her bright hair. "I'm happy to be here, too." He looked around, his gaze going dark. "Where's the snake?"

Rachel's little pointed, fuzzy ears and whiskers immediately retracted. She didn't appear to lose her good mood, however. "He... thought it wouldn't be a good idea to stay. He suspects you still don't like him much."

She didn't look like she'd be exactly heartbroken if he didn't give her the answer she hoped for, more like she would accept it and continue living her life how she chose, regardless of her brother's opinion.

TJ was impressed. She'd come a long way from the timid little thing she'd been when she and John first came here. TJ hadn't thought she'd be able to make a decision like that and stick by it with any kind of conviction before now.

"No," Matthew admitted, with all the excitement and energy of eating Brussels sprouts. "But... he treats you well?"

"Yes, very much so." A pleased flush bloomed across Rachel's rosy cheeks. Then she looked beyond Matthew's huge shoulders. TJ cringed, but she waved with her whole arm. "Hi, TJ. Hi, Steve! Are you coming over here? It's weird you're just standing way over there."

She was on a first-name basis with Steve? TJ hadn't known that she was that close with any of the other agents, but it made sense, with all the questions she'd been answering over the months.

Steve smiled pleasantly, shaking his head. "On duty, sorry."

"They need to stay there. I'm still being monitored," Matthew said.

She blinked up at her brother. "You... Oh."

She seemed disappointed but not surprised, and TJ felt like shit all over again.

The official story Rachel had been given was that Matthew had decided to turn himself in willingly. Not that FUC had found him, that TJ had ratted him out—no offense intended to rat shifters everywhere—and that there had been a chase through TJ's yard after Matthew had jumped through a window in his house in an attempt to get away.

TJ still had to clean up the glass.

"It's complicated," Matthew said, still holding Rachel's hand and shoulder. "They're here because I need to be watched for a bit, but I trust TJ's judgment."

The way Matthew glanced back at him made TJ feel like an even bigger pile of garbage.

Steve laughed, his solid hand clapping TJ's shoulder as he put on a façade for Rachel. "It's nothing major. Same thing we had to do with you. We're just making sure everyone is safe and accounted for."

"Right," Rachel said, a little too slowly. She looked at TJ one more time.

She suspected something. Rachel had been naive when she first came here, and she still could be at times, but TJ knew that look and he could tell she suspected something.

"Can I come inside? I want to see how you're being treated," Matthew said, leading Rachel to the little square house.

She brightened. "Sure! Albert set me up with some classes online, too! I'm learning how to use computers. They said I can get a job at the FUCN'A library if I get certified. Did you know he's an owl like you?"

They went inside, leaving TJ standing there with Steve, hands in his pockets, a weird, helpless feeling hitting him.

"Do we really just have to stand here?" he grouched.

It was bad enough Matthew hadn't immediately thrown him under the bus when he and Rachel started talking, but who knew what they'd be saying once they were inside, alone.

TJ didn't know Rachel that well, but he knew her well enough that he felt like he should defend his character to her. Let her know that he wasn't a total piece of garbage for betraying her brother.

"Yeah, it's kinda weird," Steve admitted. "Usually whenever we watch people, it's done from the back of a car or while I'm shifted and hiding in some shrubs."

"Yeah."

"We'll walk, circle around to the back of the house, and come back here. The wind's with us so I think we'd be able to tell if they went out the back door."

TJ hadn't thought of that, but he dismissed the possibility. "They wouldn't do that."

Rachel seemed happy and secure here and Matthew

wouldn't take her away from that. Besides, Matthew knew he couldn't hide anywhere else anymore.

"We'll do it anyway." Steve shrugged. "Consider it more experience for your future assignments."

FUC agents sometimes were assigned simple guard duty like this, but TJ had always hoped for more than standing around out in the open, just a warm body in an area in case anything were to happen.

Regardless, he was hardly in a position to complain as much as he had already, so he did as he was told, scouting the property with Steve.

He still couldn't believe Matthew wanted him around. When TJ had heard the demand while sitting behind the one-way mirror observing Steve and Sam's interrogation, he'd stood up and shouted out loud. Nolan and Albert had smacked him upside the head to promptly shut him up.

Matthew was obviously doing this to punish him. To keep an eye on him as well. *I guess it was too much to hope we could cut clean ties and go our separate ways.*

"You didn't tell us everything about what went on when you took care of him," Steve said gently on their third trip around the small, unfenced yard.

TJ's whole spine went stiff. "Yes, I did."

He was dying on that damned hill.

Except Steve was staring at him now, and it was just as bad as when any cat stared. TJ didn't look back at him, but he felt like the guy was looking into his soul and seeing everything.

Too bad it wasn't up for discussion. What had gone on between TJ and Matthew had nothing to do with FUC, or the creepy, evil fox shifter scientist, or any of those freaks who liked to kidnap people and trick them into getting these messed-up treatments.

He and Matthew got drunk together once and... something happened. But that was personal, had nothing to do with the case, and was noone's fucking business.

After his betrayal, TJ was all the more determined to keep that promise. To give Matthew *something* to prove he wasn't a piece of shit.

"If you're helping him hide his father..."

What? "I'm not helping him hide anything."

"Anything else, you mean?"

Jesus Christ. "He's not helping Bazyli. Matthew's got questions for him and probably wouldn't mind if he was found, but he has no idea where he is. I was doing my job when he was coming around, believe it or not."

"No, you weren't," Steve said, his voice incredibly even.

TJ stared at the little house FUC was renting for Rachel and John, arms crossed and refusing to look at Steve. He felt petulant, but he didn't care.

"Look, kid, I get it. I do."

"Fuck you, you do," TJ said.

"I do," Steve said. "Don't you go around repeating this, but my brother was taken when I was a little kid."

"I know. It went around the school." The information on Sam and Steve's history was pretty much common knowledge at this point.

Well, TJ hadn't known *for sure*, but it did confirm the rumors. Part of him felt a petty sort of satisfaction that the big reveal Steve thought he was letting TJ in on was already common knowledge.

"Okay, well, I was taken, too."

TJ nodded and pressed his lips together—a motion he still enjoyed, after so long of not being able to close his lips over his monstrous teeth. He looked at the man, wishing he could be tougher, that he wasn't about to give in and follow

Steve down the obvious rabbit hole he was laying out, but he was giving in.

Hard to be cold and distant when he was curious.

Steve was finally looking at him like he wasn't the shame of FUCN'A, either.

"I wanted to do all kinds of things to the woman who did this to me. Lady with bird feathers and a desperate need to steal kids and young people. Sound familiar?"

TJ's heart squeezed. "Yeah."

"It was back when your face was still..." Steve gestured vaguely at his own face, quickly dropping his hand. Like he felt bad for reminding him.

TJ shuddered. "Why are you telling me this?" He fucking hated the reminder of what he'd been. Sometimes he still felt the painful stretching and stabbing in his face. Woke up with it thinking he was back to being... that.

Back to being so ugly people avoided looking at him. Back to being so embarrassed with himself, in so much pain, that he nearly did something unforgivable just for the slightest chance at escaping it.

He hated himself for what he'd been back then.

"Because I understand the need to go about your own way to protect the people you care about. He saved your life, and you took care of him. His sister was nice to you, so you tried to hide him and get more information on your own. It wasn't bad, but you weren't doing good either, and you definitely weren't doing your job."

TJ knew it, which made it worse.

He still wasn't about to tell Steve about the things he and Matthew had talked about when they had drinks together. He especially wasn't getting into... *that*.

"I'm just saying I'm trying to look out for you. Believe it or not, I'm not judging you."

TJ rolled his eyes.

"Okay, maybe a little." Steve laughed. "The other agents are pissed off. We could've used this lead a while ago, but we don't judge. Much."

That felt... kind of good to hear. That the entire team didn't think he was an immature jackass made him feel about fifty pounds lighter.

"He was useless to you anyway," TJ tried to reason. "He's not going to lead you to his father. Is that man even his father? He must have been like Mother, right?" A woman who took in volunteers or kidnapped unwilling participants for her experiments, and then forced everyone to call her Mother.

"Nolan and Diane are doing all the tests now. And, no, you won't be given the results."

Fuck.

"It doesn't mean you won't get them. Matthew might tell you. You both seem pretty close."

TJ's throat dried up. The worst kind of heat settled into his face. He glanced at Steve, who gave him that cat look again, like he knew everything. FUC had been watching his place for a while when they'd figured out he was hiding Matthew.

Did he know?

Holy shit, he knew.

"I..."

The door suddenly opened. Rachel stepped out. Her bright red hair was now up in a high ponytail, her hands on her jean-clad hips.

"This is too weird! Steve, will you come inside already? You can spy on us in here!"

"Love to!" Steve said, moving toward the front door like there was nothing out of the ordinary.

"H-hey! Wait a minute!"

Steve stopped and looked back.

"What the fuck? What happened to following the rules and doing our job?"

Steve smiled again. "The rules don't say we can't go inside if we're invited. We've paced around enough. Besides, I'm thirsty."

Steve turned back to the house, nodding politely to Rachel as he stepped past her.

Like a friend. Or at least someone she knew well enough to let into her home and someone he trusted enough not to attack him when his back was turned.

TJ sighed. Well, he'd already broken so many rules, what was slacking off on the job this once going to hurt?

He didn't get three steps when Rachel stopped him with a hard, narrow-eyed stare.

He froze.

She didn't say a word. She eyed him up and down, all airs of friendliness gone from her.

Matthew had told her.

"You should stay here. One of you should watch the perimeter or something. That's your job, right?" she said, spinning around, marching back inside, and slamming the door behind her, not giving TJ any chance to explain himself.

He sighed and went back to his spot at the edge of the yard.

Fuck, Matthew might be keeping him close, but he was still very clearly pissed and betrayed.

TJ had no idea how long he'd be assigned to work with Matthew. They could be facing a few very long days, or worse.

TJ needed to fix this.

5

Matthew couldn't stay long.

He wished he could, but the fact that he was allowed to be here, to spend time with Rachel at all, was a generosity he hadn't expected from the likes of the Furry United Coalition.

He also hadn't expected Rachel to sing their praises the way she had when he was alone with her. Something she did before and after inviting Agent Steve into the house for coffee—as if he was a friend she had seen many times since arriving here.

"The agents here are so nice. I can show you some of the classes I'm taking. I never thought I'd get to go to school. Sometimes I even take the tests at the Academy. It's like I really get to go, even though I'm not a cadet training to become an agent."

Matthew nodded, listened to her prattle on, and was genuinely impressed with what she'd been up to. She showed him some of her notes.

He still struggled with reading, and he barely understood a lot of what she had on here.

Lot of big words.

She always had been smarter than he was.

And he was so fucking proud of her.

Then she dropped a cinder block on his head. "Have you heard anything from Dad?"

Matthew's chest went tight. The soft hope in her voice, the fragile wish that their father hadn't abandoned her... He hadn't expected it to affect him like this.

Steve was pretending to look at something on the wall, though he had to be paying attention to everything.

"No." Matthew wasn't lying. He had no doubt Rachel would believe him, too.

She did. She looked and somehow even smelled disappointed, though she took a deep breath and forced a smile. "I'm sure we'll hear from him soon."

Matthew nodded.

He wanted to speak to Bazyli. He wanted answers. Wanted to know what the hell he was doing and where he was.

Had he abandoned them? Were he and Rachel really his children?

Had he burned the compound with Matthew in it on purpose?

Thankfully, Rachel didn't make a big show of his scars. The pity in her eyes was bad enough, but she knew he wouldn't want the attention.

"They don't hurt," he finally said. "They're already fading."

That seemed to diminish the sadness in her gaze, at least marginally.

Matthew could have stayed there with her for hours, but the rain started before Steve could start making hints.

"I should go. TJ is still outside."

"He can stay in the rain a little. It won't kill him," Rachel said, her frigid words shocking the hell out of Matthew.

"No, we should go," Steve said. "Matthew's got a lot of catching up to do, and I don't want one of our agents standing out in a downpour."

It wasn't raining that hard yet, but Matthew didn't want that either. The fact that he still cared whether or not TJ got a little cold out in a summer rain annoyed him. He should hate the traitor, yet he didn't.

Rachel pressed her lips together, alarm flashing across her gaze as she looked between Steve and Matthew. "You'll keep coming back, now that you're working with FUC, right?"

"Of course I will." Matthew had no way of knowing that, but he wasn't going to worry her for no reason. "I'll be back as much as you want."

In that moment, he meant it. He didn't care what the damn rules were or who he had to answer to, or threaten; he was going to see his sister. As much as possible.

If Steve took the challenge, he didn't show it.

Rachel hugged him tight. He held her back, glaring at Steve over her shoulder.

"We'll be in touch, Rachel," Steve said, ignoring Matthew's glare. "Keep working at your studies. Our librarians, Albert and Aubrey, have been impressed and they say you'll be a great addition to the team."

"I will," Rachel muttered. She stepped back, eyes downcast, looking small and miserable.

It was stupid, but it made Matthew happy to see how much she cared.

He gripped her shoulder, giving her the biggest smile he could. "Chin up. I'll be back. I still need some lessons from you."

"Have you still been—" Rachel stopped herself, lips pursed, as if she didn't want to say it in front of Steve. Trying to protect Matthew's ego.

FUC already knew. There was no point in keeping it secret, but he still loved her all the more for watching out for him.

"TJ was helping me with the reading while I was away. We're going to resume my lessons soon."

"Oh!" Rachel's eyes popped wide. "I didn't realize." She looked thoughtful for a moment. "Maybe... we should give him a bit of a break then. For turning you in."

Matthew sighed. "I'll consider it."

It did help that the people of FUC were, so far, being decent to him. And they were certainly treating Rachel well.

He'd see where it all went, but the rain started coming down harder, and he wanted to get out to TJ before he got soaked.

He hugged his sister one more time, made another promise to return, and stepped outside with Steve.

TJ stood at the end of the driveway, under one of the tall trees there, trying to shelter himself from the coming rain. His arms were crossed. A small light glowed from the middle of his forehead. It had gotten darker since Matthew had gone inside.

None of the righteous satisfaction he thought he would feel came to him. Matthew's guts twisted with guilt instead.

"Did you get what you were looking for?" TJ directed the question to Steve.

"Yeah, she doesn't know anything."

Matthew froze. "Was that a *test*?"

He was furious, the ugly, prickling sense of betrayal rising up his chest and throat, choking him.

"Yes, it was," Steve said, walking past him. "We're already

positive that Rachel doesn't know anything about the whereabouts of your father, but it's good to confirm it from time to time. Just because she doesn't know right now doesn't mean she couldn't figure it out later."

"How long will you be checking her?"

"Until the case is closed or your father is found." Steve rubbed his hand through his hair. The lot of them were getting wet. He looked up at the sky. "She knew we'd be checking up on her from time to time. So don't worry. I doubt she'd feel tricked at this point. John has been getting the worst of it."

Matthew had almost forgotten about John. He was glad he didn't have to see the man. Not until he had a chance to get used to all this, at least.

Rachel seemed happy, but there was something sinister about the idea of anyone dating his sister. It felt like an unforgivable sin, especially for someone who'd been a person non grata, like John the cobra.

Matthew realized TJ wasn't looking at him and suspicion flared. TJ did that whenever he felt guilty.

Or was hiding something.

"You were testing me, too."

Of course they were.

TJ flinched, proving him right.

"Yup, we were." Steve cracked his knuckles. "Get over it. Let's go. I don't want to be dripping in my truck."

THEY DROVE to a small apartment building Matthew recognized.

It was in the little town just a few miles away from the Academy. He'd snuck off to this town plenty without his father noticing. It was a brick building above the laundromat, down the street from the pub.

Where he'd met TJ.

"What are we doing here?"

Steve parked the truck. He didn't kill the engine.

He twisted around in his seat, dug a jingling set of keys out from his jacket pocket, and handed them over.

Matthew took them, not understanding.

"Your apartment is number four. Don't expect much."

He still didn't get it. "Apartment?" He looked up at the building. "I'm staying here?"

"Did you think we were going to lock you in a cage?"

He did, actually.

From the wide-eyed look on TJ's face, he'd thought the same thing.

A spike of worry pierced him suddenly. TJ had aided a wanted suspect. What was to happen to him? "Is TJ going to a cage?"

"*Obviously* not," Steve snapped. He rolled his eyes. "Do you want the damn keys or not?"

"No. I don't trust you. What's this for?"

There could be a trap up there. Or there could be nothing at all. It could just be a bed to sleep in, which was more worrisome.

Father had taught him to expect no favors. If this was an attempt to lower his guard, he wouldn't fall for it.

He'd already made that mistake.

"Jesus Christ," Steve muttered. "This isn't charity, all right? You're officially working for us now, and you need a place to stay. Your first month is paid for, so any earnings you receive after today you need to save for your next month if you choose to stay."

"I work for you?" *What?*

"Temporarily, yes. You're going to be paid for your services. Don't get any ideas," Steve said. "There's no cameras hidden in there, but we're still keeping an eye on you."

"What will I be doing?"

"Right now? It's just information. This is all touch and go, you'll get more notes later. This is all temporary."

It was too much.

A place to stay? And a job? Even a temporary one…

The agents of FUC had cared for Rachel and John until they could get on their feet, but now that Matthew thought of it, he didn't know what John was doing for money either. Rachel was likely going to be working for FUC in some capacity. John already had training. Was he working for them, too?

"You want the apartment, or are you just going to sit there staring at me?"

"No, I'll go. Thank you." He glanced at TJ.

He wanted to say… He wasn't sure what he wanted to say.

He didn't want to leave the guy with Agent Steve, though.

He had no choice.

Matthew left the truck.

Steve didn't wait for anything else to happen. He immediately drove away, his tires kicking up a wave of rainwater, leaving Matthew standing there, still unable to believe it.

The fob beeped and actually unlocked the door, letting him inside to a set of stairs.

He climbed them. No one told him to leave. No one was there at all.

Room four. He inserted the key.

The door unlocked.

He didn't step inside.

This felt... weird. Matthew poked his head in and glanced around.

It was a simple, studio apartment. Made sense that FUC wouldn't put too much money or resources into him, but it was more than he was used to.

He felt like he was breaking into someone else's home.

He was used to staying in cabins and shacks he'd busted into. Sleeping in dusty beds or corners. Whenever he wasn't staying with TJ, of course.

Even those lodgings had seemed luxurious compared to his time in the bunker. Underground. Damp. Cold. The sunlight streaming through a broken window on a warm day in a fisherman's shack, the sound of crickets chirping, had felt magical.

Waking in TJ's small home with the scent of coffee and cooking bacon had been divine.

This... He would likely be more impressed if the weather was better.

It was cold, the walls as gray as the sky outside. It wasn't a cage, but he decided to perform a sweep for bugs before he would feel grateful.

He searched every inch of the apartment. The vents, the legs of the cot, behind the bathroom mirror, everywhere. He wasn't very smart, but he knew what surveillance looked like.

Nothing.

Nothing but a slightly off-putting smell.

Unbelievable.

Was this small space really for him?

The kitchen was most interesting to him. It consisted of a single countertop with a sink, a mini fridge, and a double-element burner he could plug in. There were two cupboards. Inside one was a mishmash of plates, cups, and bowls. They didn't match, but he didn't expect them to. In the drawer was cutlery, also from different sets and scratched with age.

That sense of gratitude he'd refused to feel was suddenly hitting him.

These were for him. He didn't care they were likely someone's throwaways or that they were chipped and cracked. Someone had given them to him.

In the lower cupboards beneath the counter there was a single deep pot and a jar of instant coffee with a kettle. A small bag of dry rice, a few ramen packets, and a box of cereal sat next to them. A bottle of dish soap with a single roll of paper towels were behind those.

He didn't dare hope for much when he opened the little fridge, but any expectations he'd built up were exceeded when he found what he did.

Milk and creamer waited for him, along with a paper bag. Inside, a carton of bacon, eggs, a bag of bread, and a pack of chicken thighs.

Along with a note from his sister.

I would have grabbed more, but you gave me such short notice! I had to order online; the receipt is here. John delivered it. If something is missing from the order, or if you need anything else, let me know. And come over for supper whenever you want! I love you. I can't wait to talk to you more.

Rachel.

His throat closed. At least now he knew what that off-putting scent had been. John had been in here, but Mathew couldn't be annoyed, even knowing he owed the man a thank-you for his trouble.

He was supposed to be the one to protect his sister, but

she was the one looking out for him. Providing. Giving him this food.

She was feeding him when he was lying to her, still keeping from her that Bazyli Smith was, more than likely, not her father.

And he was not her brother.

She still felt like a sister. Like someone he loved and wanted to protect.

He still wasn't too sure about FUC, but whatever opportunities they provided him, he wouldn't waste them.

For her sake, he would make this work, and when the time came to tell her the truth, when he knew everything there was to know and there were no longer any doubts, he would ensure her pain would be minimal.

Though, despite his new lease on his current situation, as he prepared some spicy ramen, he couldn't help but wish TJ were here.

6

TJ had no idea what he expected when he knocked on Matthew's door.

The cowardly part of him sure didn't think the man would answer, and when he did, the door yanking open like the giant maw of Aladdin's cave whooshing open before him...he was struck dumb.

The surprise on Matthew's face immediately transformed into a barely simmering tolerance. "What are you doing here?"

"Uh..." TJ had to clear his suddenly dry throat. He lifted the bag. "House-warming gift?"

Matthew barely moved. He glanced down at the bag then at TJ, and he didn't say a word.

It was kind of annoying.

"Just let me explain, and if it's not good enough, I'll leave you alone. You owe me that much."

"I do?"

"*Yeah.*" Now TJ was positively pissed. "I took care of you after the fire, and then I didn't say anything about you to anyone, even though you kept coming back to me. You told me yourself you would've let your dad lock me in a cage if he wanted to, and the worst thing I ever did was tell the higher-ups at FUC where you were after months of being at large. Yes, you fucking owe me."

He hadn't meant to say all that, but it was out, and the shocked look on Matthew's face suggested that he might have gotten his point across.

Matthew stepped aside, and TJ entered.

The space was small. FUC didn't have unlimited resources, but he'd expected... something more than this. The room TJ got when he was recovering from his own procedures had been more luxurious.

"Wow."

"What was that?"

"Nothing." TJ quickly removed his shoes. It felt weird being in a space that belonged to Matthew, instead of the other way around.

"I'm sorry, were you making dinner?" He then smelled warm spices coming from the joke of a kitchen—more of a hotel kitchenette, really. He saw the steaming water. Something was cooking on the elements. Soup, it seemed.

Matthew cursed, rushing to the elements and turning one down before his little pot could boil over. "Yes, well, trying. I'm not much of a cook."

TJ finally noticed the little ramen pack next to the element.

"FUC stockpiled you with some stuff? That's good."

"No, well, maybe some of it, but my sister purchased a few things and had them delivered when she found out I was coming to see her."

A soft, painful squeeze caught TJ in the chest. A bit of jealousy that Matthew actually had someone who cared enough to do that. That he still *had* family.

And a sense of hurt that he hadn't been given more.

"Well, if you like, do you want to show me what you got? I brought some things, but maybe I can help you out."

Matthew glanced back at him. There was no trace of that distrust and irritation from before, though he was still cautious. "Thank you. That would be nice of you."

TJ stepped forward. He placed the little bag on the counter, quickly showing Matthew the contents. It wasn't much. He'd expected this place to have some things, after all, but now that he saw how sparse the place was, he wished he'd brought more.

"I, uh, bought you this one from the store, thought it would be fun." He handed the box over. A gift set of hot sauces. *Smack Yo Mama Hot, Ass Burnin' Hot, Melt Your Tongue Off Heat!*

Matthew struggled to read, but after a quick squint, he actually snorted a laugh at the names. "Really? Am I reading this right?"

"Probably." TJ already felt lighter with that smile. He pulled out a few more items. Hand towels for his bathroom. A shaving gift, since he was always using TJ's cream and spare razors.

And the Jack Ryan book from TJ's house.

Matthew took it in both hands, looked at it, then at TJ. "You're giving me this?"

"You're the only one who bothered to read it." TJ found himself leaning a little more toward the fantasy stuff and was currently getting through the second book in the Witcher series.

He'd bought the Jack Ryan, but it couldn't hold his attention. More than once, he'd caught Matthew squinting his way and mouthing out the words slowly on the couch.

"It's yours. I don't even know if you've got a radio or whatever in here, but you need something to do."

Matthew's throat worked in a soft swallow. "Thank you." He set the book aside. The air suddenly felt heavy between them again but for an entirely different reason.

"I also got this." TJ pulled out the six-pack of beer. "To celebrate your new place."

"Even though I'm bad at holding my alcohol?"

TJ's face heated, a flash of what happened the last time. "Well, no one's perfect."

He handed Matthew a can, as if to prove it.

"Now step aside before you overcook those noodles."

"I can figure out noodles."

"Yeah, but these are plain." TJ looked into the pot. "You got anything else in the fridge?"

"Some breakfast and dinner supplies."

TJ helped himself to looking. He immediately pulled out two eggs. "It's too late to cook the chicken, but you can spruce up these noodles you know? This is how a college student eats them."

"I've never been to college."

"That you know of," TJ said.

"I can barely read. I doubt I went to high school, let alone a college."

Right. TJ swallowed around his embarrassment and got to work. "Watch this."

After checking the noodles were still al dente, he turned the burner back up a little, bringing it to a boil before cracking two eggs inside to let them cook in the boiling water.

"Next time you should cook those chicken thighs, with the skin on, then shred it and dump the chicken, skin, and grease into the pot. It makes the noodles even more amazing."

"I didn't know you knew cooking. You always ordered takeout when I came over."

That was pretty much how he lived normally, too. "This doesn't really count as cooking. If Diane knew I was dumping chicken grease into my ramen, she'd kill me, too. But I can't help it; it's good. Pro-tip though. When you cook your bacon tomorrow, cook your eggs in the hot grease right after then toast your bread in what's left over in the pan when you're done. *That's* amazing."

"That sounds disgusting!" Matthew said, but was full-on laughing now.

God, that felt good. This was what TJ wanted. For Matthew to not hate him. To treat him like... what? A friend again?

Like someone that he wouldn't glare at, at least.

"We should add some of your hot sauce," Matthew said, looking over the bottles.

TJ tensed up. *We?*

"I think I'd like to try the Smack Yo Mama," Matthew said, carefully reading the words. "How about you?"

As in, he wanted TJ to eat with him?

That sounded nice, but he wasn't sure about the hot sauce. TJ was a wuss when it came to spice, and he never thought people actually bought those gift set bottles to use them.

Not that he was going to back down since Matthew was in such a good mood.

"Yeah, that sounds all right," he said.

Matthew grabbed a small spoon, which was a relief until Matthew used that single spoonful on himself, tasting what was inside.

Then TJ watched in horror as the guy apparently liked it so much that he dumped almost half the bottle into the pot.

TJ was so fucked. "Won't that be too hot?"

"It's barely hot," Matthew said, "But tasty."

"Oh!" That was a relief. "Well, sorry it was false advertising, but at least you said it tastes good. Some companies like to hide the taste of their sauces with the heat."

"I see,"" Matthew said, frowning. "Well, it's good to know these should be good. I'm more eager to try these noodles now than I was before, even if it won't be spicy."

Two minutes later they were sitting on the floor under the window, bowls in hand. Matthew slurped down the contents of his bowl like it was absolutely nothing.

TJ's mouth was on fire.

He was dying.

Holy shit, this is the worst, and he'd only had a single bite.

Matthew had already eaten his noodles and egg, and now he held the bowl to his lips and slurped down the rest of the juice like it wasn't literally lava.

What the fuck?

"Ah, that was very good. Thank you." Matthew looked at him, his smile vanishing. "You... Are you okay?"

"Yeah." TJ coughed, reaching for his cold beer, which did next to nothing to chase away the heat. "Fine."

"Did you choke?" Matthew seemed genuinely concerned. "Your face and ears are red."

TJ shook his head. "I think a little went down the wrong pipe. That your bathroom?" He set his bowl down without waiting for an answer, rushing inside.

His nose was leaking like crazy. He blew it then stuck his face under the tiny sink and opened his mouth to the water, making it as cold as he could get it.

Matthew wasn't a man. Not even a shifter. He was some otherworldly thing if he could handle *that*. Jesus.

Matthew didn't knock to check on him. TJ was thankful for that much. He composed himself as best he could, his mouth still tingling with unpleasant heat, but at least now he thought he could talk right, and his face didn't look like a stoplight in the mirror.

He stepped out.

His heart fluttered in a flurry of scared little ripples as Matthew helped himself to a second bowl.

The man grinned at him as he went to sit on the floor again. "Too hot for you?"

TJ glared at him. He wanted to lie. Sooooo badly. But it was obvious.

He coughed and it felt like he was drooling fire. "You're a robot in disguise if you can handle that."

Matthew actually laughed at him. The jerk. Worse, he looked right at TJ as he slurped back another big, long trail of noodles, chewing slowly before swallowing it all down like it was nothing.

"You're such a baby."

"*What*?"

"You." Matthew pointed his fork at him. "You're a big baby."

"Whatever."

He couldn't eat any more, but he didn't want to leave either. And since Matthew wasn't kicking him out, TJ went to sit next to him on the floor, leaning against the wall.

They said nothing for a bit. Matthew kept eating until he was done. Then he set his bowl aside and wiped his mouth with the back of his large hand.

"I really didn't want to give you up, you know."

Matthew said nothing.

"I'm not lying."

A heavy sigh. "Yeah, I know. Still mad at you." Matthew brought his knee up to scratch it then picked some invisible lint off his pants. "You could have told me something was about to happen. I would'nt've run."

TJ looked at him.

Matthew rolled his eyes. "Shut up. I'm serious."

"You would have stuck around if I told you FUC had been watching us for a while and was planning on coming in to arrest you? Really?"

"Yes, asshole, really." Matthew glared at him. "I wasn't gonna leave you out to dry like that."

Matthew looked, and sounded, like he really meant it. Like he was insulted TJ didn't have more faith in him. It made TJ kind of ashamed of himself.

"Was it because I kissed you?"

TJ froze.

Matthew nodded, seemingly taking the silence for something it wasn't. "It was because of that."

"No!" TJ slammed his hands on the floor, like he was about to shoot to his feet or... do *something*. He wasn't sure what.

There wasn't much he could do.

"I... No, it wasn't because of that."

Matthew lifted a brow, like he didn't believe him.

"It *wasn't*," TJ insisted. "Is that what you've been thinking?"

"You kicked me out of your house when it happened, and last time I decided to come back. you wouldn't let me have a beer from your fridge, and then FUC picked me up. What was I supposed to think?"

Fair enough, he supposed. Miserable heat flushed into TJ's cheeks. The memory of that night was... not the best.

They'd been outside in TJ's backyard, and, yeah, they both had some drinks. Not many, but TJ had been amused at how Matthew could hardly seem to handle a few beers. The guy was tough. He was strong in ways TJ couldn't fathom, loyal to his sister, and he'd been through all kinds of shit, but he was a total lightweight.

They'd sat side by side, their shoulders not quite touching, while they looked up at the stars. Matthew seemed to know what each one was and had been shocked when TJ couldn't even point out the most well-known of them.

"How do you not know what the North Star is?"

"Why does it matter?" Another beer can hissed as TJ cracked it open. "I'm not about to go into the bushes anytime soon."

Matthew rolled his eyes. "You never plan these things. You always need a way to track where you are and where you're going."

TJ wanted to ask if these were lessons from his father. He decided he didn't want to spoil the mood. It had been kind of nice, sitting there, listening to Matthew bitch about how TJ had so much knowledge available to him and didn't even know the locations and names of the stars. Meanwhile, Matthew would struggle to read the names of some of those same constellations.

They were working on that. TJ tried to encourage Matthew into a little light reading when he came over.

"What are their names then?"

"What?" Matthew blinked at him, his breath smelling a little of beer.

For some reason, TJ inched closer so that their shoulders touched. "Tell me what they are and quit complaining. What's that one?"

He pointed to some random, bright star in the sky.

"That's not a star; that's a planet."

TJ rolled his eyes. "All right, fine. What planet is it?" He took another drink.

For several minutes, it was quiet, save for the crickets, and then Matthew's calm, even voice as he rattled off the planets and constellations. TJ didn't remember hardly any of them.

Something changed. He was so focused on the sound of Matthew's voice and the warmth of his shoulder that he nearly fell asleep against the man.

Matthew said something, and TJ looked at him.

TJ couldn't remember if he did it first, or if Matthew initiated it, but the man's mouth was on his.

And then everything went to pot.

"Hey, are you even listening?" Matthew shoved his shoulder, jostling him.

TJ pulled back, putting more distance between them.

"Sorry."

He rubbed at his eyes, his mouth tingling in a weird, phantom memory. He felt Matthew staring at him but TJ couldn't look back at him.

Matthew made an impatient sound. "Right."

"No! It's not... *Fuck*." He didn't know what to say. He wasn't sure how he was supposed to fix this. "It definitely wasn't because of that, though. I swear."

Matthew seemed to relax a little. "You swear?"

"Yeah." TJ swallowed, realizing he was digging his nails into his knees. That hurt, so he stopped.

"I, uh, figured out after the fact that..." Matthew mumbled. "I mean I always knew..."

TJ frowned. He'd only known Matthew a little while. The last time the guy struggled with his words this badly was right after he'd pulled TJ out of the blazing compound.

"What?" he asked. "You knew what?"

Matthew brought his knees up, his elbows resting there

while he scrubbed his hand behind his neck. His cheeks suddenly looked a little pink.

"I *knew* that boys kissing boys wasn't exactly common, but I never... I wasn't thinking. I know now that lots of guys don't really like that sort of thing. So I'm sorry. There."

He reached for his drink. He took a long swig. Like he was trying to hide his face.

Oh.

Jesus Christ, now TJ was feeling a little warm. "Uh, yeah. Right. Thanks for that."

Matthew grunted.

This probably meant Matthew had been the one to initiate it. All sorts of questions flew through TJ's head.

Why? Why would Matthew do that? Did he regret it? Was he just curious?

Did any of that even matter?

And what did TJ think about it?

"You were the first person to kiss me, you know?"

Matthew looked at him, blinked, then grinned. "Yeah, right."

"You don't believe me?"

"I've never kissed anyone before, but I figured you..." Matthew waved his hand in TJ's general direction, as if that was supposed to mean something. "I mean you're so..."

"I know you saw the pictures of what I used to look like."

Matthew froze.

"Did I look very kissable to you then?"

"Well, no. I guess not. You'd give whoever was kissing you about a dozen lip piercings if you tried."

TJ jerked back. Then he laughed.

An actual belly laugh.

He'd never laughed about anything involving the way he used to look. There was never anything funny to him about that. He'd hated how he looked, was disgusted by himself and the things he was willing to do to fix it.

But Matthew's comment was kind of funny.

And Matthew was grinning at him, like he was proud of the joke he clearly hadn't meant to say.

TJ kind of wanted to wipe that smug look off his face.

So he leaned in and kissed the guy.

7

Matthew was surprised, but not in a bad way.

He didn't think it would ever happen again. He sure as hell didn't think TJ would be the one to do it.

It was barely a kiss—not that he had much experience in these things. It was more of a press of their mouths before TJ pulled back.

He wiped his lips with the back of his hand, took a quick drink, and tried not looking at Matthew.

"So, uh, yeah." TJ's cheeks turned pink. A soft light glowed at the center of his forehead. He cursed, rubbing at the spot before it could form a lure, which would branch out from his forehead and hang like a Christmas light. "Stupid light."

"No," Matthew said. He grabbed TJ's arm, yanking him forward, overcome with a new surge of confidence as he put his hand on the back of TJ's head and kissed him again.

Deeper this time. Probably a little sloppily.

TJ didn't seem to care. He leaned into it, shooting a rush of excited energy through Matthew's body.

This... felt nice. More than nice. It was warm and inviting, and Matthew's hands seemed to move of their own accord. His palms found TJ's narrow waist. The guy was thinner than he was, but the more Matthew touched, the more he realized how solid TJ was. He felt firm muscle and warm skin through the guy's shirt.

He didn't want to feel through his shirt, though. Matthew stuck his hand under the material, searching for skin.

Felt good. TJ shuddered, his mouth opening.

Matthew moaned. Even better.

He pushed his tongue inside, searching, not entirely sure what he was doing, but it seemed that as long as he wasn't thinking too hard about it, he was doing it right, because TJ wasn't complaining.

Until it stopped.

TJ's hands, his long, strong fingers, pushed against Matthew's chest.

Matthew stopped. TJ didn't exactly yank himself away. He didn't get up without a word and walk off the way he had when Matthew first kissed him under the stars, but the kissing, as pleasant as it was, was over.

TJ seemed to be thinking. Matthew would give anything to know what he was thinking about.

"Does it disgust you?"

TJ shook his head. "No. Uh, you?"

Matthew shook his head. "No."

He frowned. "Are you sure you've never kissed anyone before? You were pretty good at it."

Matthew snorted, but he smiled. "Yeah, well, maybe I'm a born natural. The only person around me was Bobby, and there was no way anything was going to happen there."

TJ shuddered. "Makes sense. Then there's your sister,

your dad, and the other goons in there. What were their names again?"

"I don't think it matters," Matthew said, all warm and fuzzy.

Matthew liked this. This felt easy. The anger he felt at TJ earlier was pretty much gone, and their friendship seemed like it was back to before.

Then TJ shattered it. "You gotta be, what? Twenty-five? You could even be older than that. And you don't remember anything before your dad woke you up when you were sick. Maybe you've got someone out there."

It was spoken so softly. Carefully.

Matthew didn't want to consider it, but he did.

And deep down, a piece of him rejected the thought.

"No, it... doesn't feel right."

TJ tilted his head.

Matthew shrugged. "I just... I don't think there was anyone else. I don't feel like I'm missing a friend... or a lover."

"Lover?"

Was that the wrong word to use?

"Do you want to stay the night?" He had no experience that he could remember, but he wasn't stupid. He knew what he was asking for.

TJ knew it, too. "Kinda curious, not gonna lie."

"But you're not staying." It wasn't a question. TJ was doing that thing he did again when he didn't want to look at him. "It's all right. I understand. With our luck, those suck-up FUC agents probably got this place bugged."

"Did you do a sweep?"

Matthew took another drink. His can was empty. "Every inch, but like you said, these people find a way."

And he sure as hell didn't want to risk a bunch of shithead agents hearing him fumbling around and making an ass of himself. He'd rather save the fumbling for when he knew he could be alone with TJ.

And he wanted to be alone with him.

So much.

"I should go." TJ stood. Matthew stood with him, following him to the door.

"Will you come back?" Jesus, that sounded so desperate and pathetic.

TJ didn't act like it was desperate or pathetic.

"Yeah. I mean...I think so." He opened the door. "If you're okay with it, and if FUC allows it, you can come back to my house if you want, too. I don't think they bugged my house."

He frowned, as though giving it serious consideration.

Matthew didn't want to think about it either.

"Either way," TJ said, as if dismissing the unwelcome thoughts of being spied on. "You're probably going to get a visit from FUC long before I can come back. They're going to want you to help them."

If it meant he could be free, and see more of TJ, he was all right with that.

Though he didn't want to let the man go.

Matthew hadn't been entirely happy when TJ showed up at his door, but now he hated the fact that TJ was leaving.

And when he was gone, the tiny apartment felt even smaller.

DIANE WAS TIRED. The screen was starting to hurt her eyes, and soon, she was going to need more than a pair of reading glasses to get through her day.

A lack of a proper social life and a love for her job meant she was in the clinic later than even the custodians. There was always more paperwork to be done.

A notification popped up on the top right-hand side of her screen. Matthew's test results were back.

Weird timing. The guys in the lab must be doing some overtime, too.

She sighed, wanting a break from looking over incident reports, X-rays from a few broken bones, and updates on the few shifter pregnancies there were to keep an eye on.

Finding out who Matthew was related to and locating the potential family was something different. It wasn't always good news. The times when the family wanted nothing to do with the people FUC found was always a sad affair.

Or when there was no family at all.

She opened the report and immediately scanned down to the match section. It was positive. Matthew had family.

Diane squinted at the screen.

No way was she reading that right. She reached for her glasses, put them on, and scanned the document again.

She heaved a sigh, falling back in her chair. It was too late for this nonsense. She was going home, and in the morning, she was going to have to get the blood test done again. Someone had mixed up the samples. Ran a series of tests under Matthew's name with blood from one of Diane's regulars.

One of the Huntlys. She knew Albert—FUC's resident librarian—and she knew Beverly—Albert's wife, who taught at the Academy. They brought Finn—their toddler son—in for checkups plenty of times over the last two years.

How did some of that little boy's blood from his last checkup end up being tested instead of Matthew's?

That must be what had happened, because Matthew had nothing to do with the Huntly family. There was no way, and she was too tired to want to handle this tonight.

Diane sent off a quick message to the labs, letting them know of the error and saying they would have to redo the test with a fresh sample and search the database again tomorrow.

She left the office before she could see the annoyed reply.

8

TJ hadn't seen or heard from Matthew since the night they kissed.

Fuck, had it really been a week already?

Yeah, he looked over at the calendar hanging on the kitchen wall, fingers clenching on the table. It had been the longest week of his life, especially after that kiss and how they seemed to work a few things out. Not to mention FUC had been up his ass the entire time.

He grabbed his pen, twiddling it between his fingers, trying to pay attention to what was in front of him, which was boring as all hell. His suspension had ended prematurely, the excuse was a lack of staff since everyone seemed to be finding mates and having babies, and more resources were being put into finding Matthew's father, which meant Rachel and Matthew were being watched more closely.

Not that they trusted TJ to be out in the field, especially as a newbie. They needed him to handle paperwork, which he now had flying out of his ears. Not even anything fun, either. No, he was supposed to go over the expense reports, as if he worked in accounting or something. His only job was to go over the reports and double-check that everything added up the way those accounting nerds said it was supposed to be.

So he spent a lot of time with the calculator app on his phone, signing his initials to make sure he did what he was supposed to, and moving on to the next page. They didn't have desk space for him on campus so he was working from home for the moment, which suited him just fine.

He tapped off his calculator and checked his actual phone.

No missed calls. Nothing from Matthew.

He got back to work.

Exciting stuff.

Maybe it would have been more interesting if he could see what salaries individual agents were being paid, but no. He wasn't even getting that. It was the budgets for new computers. The money used for food for the FUCN'A's cafeteria, new chairs and desks, window repairs after one shifter accidentally blew up a lab. Even updated gym equipment and landscaping around the facility itself.

He almost wished he could catch someone laundering money. *Anything* was better than this.

He still felt Matthew's mouth burning on his. He still thought about it at night, was still distracted by the memory of it when he was supposed to be working. Supposed to be making good with FUCN'A after his massive fuckup.

Work that should only take an hour or two took several.

Matthew might not be calling, but from what he'd heard, FUC agents were calling on him. They were putting him to work, making him answer questions, holding interrogations that lasted for several hours at a time.

TJ had heard they'd taken Matthew on location to the old facility a few times so he could give them tours now that the place was no longer on fire. The FUC agents were looking for anything they could, any extra piece of information that could lead them to Matthew's father or to more answers about the bird woman, Mother. They wanted to find out why there were so many kidnappings, so many experiments.

TJ wished it would all be over.

And he wished his eyes wouldn't cross when he looked over these fucking papers anymore.

Screw this.

He started signing his initials on the remaining pages.

He didn't read them. He didn't care anymore. He wasn't an accountant, and if there were any errors, they could take this up with that department.

TJ scanned the papers on his phone and emailed them back, shooting to his feet. He grabbed his keys from the hook and rushed to the front door.

He opened it and stopped. Froze.

Matthew stood there, his hand raised like he was about to knock.

They stared at each other for a few seconds.

"You came?" TJ asked dumbly.

"Uh, yeah. Well..." Matthew glanced back, and TJ realized someone was with him.

Sam, the cat shifter. House cat, not anything wild like his bobcat brother. The man wasn't wearing a suit, but he looked dressed for being out and about.

"Good to see you're done with the expense reports," Sam said. "Come on. You're needed."

"Needed where?" TJ frowned, shaking off the irritation that Matthew couldn't be here alone, and stepped out. He shut the door behind him.

"Where do you think?" Sam asked, though not unkindly.

"Matt asked, and we agreed. You were in that facility, too. Maybe there's something you'll notice when you're there."

He blinked, the realization taking an embarrassing amount of time to sink in. "You want me to go back? I was barely there any time at all. I wouldn't know my way around."

"That's what literally everyone said, but he's insisting." Sam gestured to Matthew. "Besides, we could use some extra hands, and you're probably sick of the paperwork."

He was. He would so rather Matthew had snuck off to see him so they could figure out... whatever was going on with them, but that apparently wasn't happening right now, and he was itching to do something of substance.

"All right, of course. I'm there. We taking separate cars?"

"No, I'm driving," Sam said, turning back to the truck parked right behind TJ's. "Otherwise, we would've called you."

He was kind of annoyed by the babysitting, but he let it go, climbing into the back of the cab. Matthew sat up front with Sam.

TJ stared at the back of Matthew's head. The guy barely looked at him. What was going on? Was there something TJ should be worried about here?

Was he making something out of nothing?

It took about thirty minutes to drive to the compound. By truck, it was barely the distance from FUCN'A, where TJ had spent so much of his time over the last few years, but no one in town would just stumble across it.

No one human, anyway.

Sam took a turn onto a dirt road that was barely visible from the two-lane highway. Overhanging tree branches and wild shrubs made it look as though there was almost nothing there. Those same branches reached out and scratched the glass and sides of the truck as Sam drove through them before the way cleared just enough for the truck to bump and dip the rest of the way down the lane.

Another five minutes of that and then TJ could smell water through the open window. He thought it might have something to do with his shifter type. He always seemed to be drawn to the creeks and rivers. Any body of water where he could swim pulled him in.

Then they arrived.

He didn't like being back here. He could almost feel the heat licking at his skin and clothes before Matthew threw them into the river.

It wasn't the first time he'd been back since escaping that day of the fire, but it looked completely different. More trees had been cleared, making room for more FUC equipment. People were scattered all over the place. Trailers and lights were set up for working after dark.

Even now, as Sam parked his truck in the designated space for vehicles, TJ could see agents of FUC, wearing special suits, gloves, and booties to cover their shoes, pulling burned equipment out from the holes in the ground they'd made.

TJ got a move on, exiting the truck after Sam and Matthew. "They're still pulling from the compound?" He hadn't known that. He'd figured the place was still of interest, but this was a full-on hot spot.

"We found a few rooms that weren't as badly burned. It's like a honeycomb down there," Sam said, shrugging. "Though they usually are. The people who built these places are like moles."

Yeah, that was true. So many of these things kept popping up it was almost a joke at this point. And it wasn't even the first compound that TJ had been imprisoned in.

Maybe the real reason TJ didn't like it here had more to do with the fact that he'd been locked up in one of these himself and less to do with the fire that nearly killed him and Matthew.

Sam nodded to Matthew. "He requested your assistance."

TJ glanced at Matthew, who stuffed his hands into his pockets and pursed his lips.

"Okay?"

"There a problem?" Sam asked.

"I just... No. I'm here to help. I'll do whatever you want me to do."

"Good. Get some gloves and sign in over there. You'll be digging through the debris, taking photos. You're not to move anything, though. We got other guys taking care of that."

"Got it." TJ moved to do as he was told. He'd never had this sort of assignment before. Though he'd barely had any since finishing his courses at FUCN'A. He was still a rookie.

Seemed simple enough stuff so far, however. He checked in and showed his ID and badge to the guy behind the folding table. He got a few raised brows, and there were clearly some whispers.

Right. People were still wondering how it was he had a job when he'd helped Matthew hide for so long.

Whatever. Not his problem. He got a lanyard to show he was allowed to be on-site, a face mask, some instructions on where they were to go and what they were going to be doing, and that was it. He was allowed in. Just like that.

It almost seemed too easy. Like something else was going on.

He headed toward the entrance. It wasn't the same one he

and Matthew had escaped from. That was right on the water. This was a larger cave entrance. He remembered vehicles being here. Not many and not all of them had seemed workable.

Now, the garage was empty, the door completely taken off. By the explosion or by FUC, he didn't know.

"Your heart's beating fast," Matthew said, keeping his voice low as they passed by a dozen or more other agents in the garage, heading deeper into the pit. "You all right?"

"Fine." TJ's throat was dry as hell. He wiped his hands on his jeans. They were just a little sweaty.

Matthew noticed. "Are you scared?"

"No. Shut up. Let's go. How many levels down did they say?"

"Fourth floor down."

That wasn't too bad. There were agents everywhere, and Matthew was with him. TJ trusted him.

He could do this.

Amazingly, the elevator actually worked. One of them did, at least. It had either been repaired or hadn't sustained enough damage to worry anyone using it. He saw agents stepping in and out of it without a problem. The doors didn't seem to open and close, though. A rope was used to tie off the door so no one would stupidly step into the shaft by mistake.

Not that TJ stepped into it or wanted to.

Matthew grabbed his elbow, directing him toward the stairs.

TJ was kind of relieved for that. Matthew probably only did it because of his clear nerves.

Made him want to kiss the guy again.

There were lights strewn around the facility. Dozens of power cords from FUC's generators were everywhere, which was good. TJ had been worried they'd be working in the dark.

It still smelled like gas, and that smell just got worse the deeper in they went. He had to put on his mask.

Matthew did the same.

"So, what've they had you doing?"

"Mostly airlifting heavy material back to the Academy," Matthew said. "The lab is for students, but it's the closest one they have. Anything they can't work on, I load into trucks or cans, and they're taken to other FUC locations."

Made sense. Matthew was a huge owl shifter and could be useful that way. TJ was kind of jealous about that. God, how amazing would that be, to fly?

"This is the one," Matthew said, yanking TJ from his thoughts.

TJ nearly jumped.

It was as brightly lit down here as it was on the top floor. All artificial white lights but fewer people. TJ could mostly hear the sounds of other people echoing through the facility as pipes were banged against, voices traveling distantly through the few vents that weren't blocked.

The air felt more stale down here. The scent of sweat and something else was heavy and close.

"We're heading to a lab Father never used. He said he never used it, anyway," Matthew said, rushing ahead.

No chitchat. He was barely looking at TJ at all.

Then TJ understood.

Matthew didn't avoid the elevator for TJ's benefit. He avoided it for himself.

He was nervous. More so than TJ.

TJ hurried to catch up. "Hey, you good?" he asked.

Matthew didn't stop moving. "Yes, perfect. We're almost there."

Okay.

TJ didn't say anything. For now. There might be other people around. Maybe it was personal, but knowing Matthew was getting the shakes suddenly made TJ feel better about being in another depressing hole.

Maybe that was why he started talking.

"The place where they found me was similar to this."

Matthew looked at him sharply. TJ couldn't see his mouth with the mask, but his eyes were wide.

"You..." Matthew shook himself. "Yes, of course. I'm sorry. I shouldn't have asked you to—"

"No." TJ grabbed Matthew's shoulder before he could stop himself. Squeezed it then let go. "I want to be here. This is fine."

He got it now. FUC didn't need him on-site. Matthew asked for him to be here because he was the one getting wigged out by being in his father's bunker again.

"At least this place didn't have as many people getting mutilated," TJ said, trying to make a joke of it.

His words felt as stale and horrible as the air around him.

"I mean it's nice to be able to look through all this junk and know there's not a hundred people waiting for FUC to dig through it all for some answers."

"There might have been, at one point," Matthew said. "I have no memories of it when it was fully functional, but it easily could have been used as a prison for humans and shifters alike. Perhaps you were kept here at some point before being relocated to the other compound."

That was something TJ had already thought of, and he dismissed it quickly. "Nah, I don't think so. I mean I was always pretty drugged up, but I don't remember ever being moved, and the guys at FUC would've figured it out if I came from another place a long time ago."

"Hmm," Matthew said, noncommittal.

"Can I ask why you're so nervous to be back down here?"

TJ had his own reasons, but Matthew had lived in this place. He'd left it and returned freely whenever he could get away with it.

Matthew glanced up to the ceiling. What was left of it. TJ was pretty sure there used to be ceiling tiles before they burned away, leaving the pipes and vents exposed.

"The barrels are gone," Matthew said. He touched the side of his jaw, where, under his mask, stretched some of his burn scars. "They weren't everywhere, but there were some on each floor. Supposed to be used for backup power." Matthew shook his head. "Instead, Father was going to use them as a last resort. Emptied them all through the fire system and burned everything. I keep thinking that the deeper we get, maybe there's some gasoline still left. Hard to get out when you go so deep down."

Jesus.

"Maybe we should get out of here." TJ grabbed Matthew's elbow, ready to drag him back to the stairs if he had to.

Matthew yanked his arm out of TJ's grasp. "No. I want to stay, to prove that I'm cooperating."

"You don't have to do *this*. They can assign you something else. You don't owe anyone here."

"Yes, I do," Matthew said, a flash in his eyes. "If my cooperation means Rachel is continually treated well and means you can keep your job..."

TJ blinked. "I... You're worried about that?"

"You should be, too." Matthew started moving again. TJ followed him.

"You've been here for five minutes, and there are already whispers about you. About what you did."

"I don't care what they think."

"I *do*," Matthew snapped, a conviction in his voice that almost stopped TJ in his tracks. "You saved my life and kept my secret."

TJ didn't correct Matthew that *he'd* saved TJ's life first. The guy seemed determined.

"I will prove myself trustworthy. For Rachel and for you. If I can give them something... maybe they will see your faith in me, that your efforts and your willingness to wait before turning me in weren't for nothing." Matthew stopped and looked right at him. "That you're a good agent with good judgment."

Wow. Okay. That was... TJ was touched in a way he'd never been before. He felt actually kind of bashful as he rubbed the back of his neck, unable to hold Matthew's gaze. "Jeez, if you wanted to kiss me again, you could just ask."

Matthew blinked.

"You don't gotta go through this song and dance about what a good agent I am."

Because he clearly was not. Those people were right to whisper about him. He'd fucked up.

Though that wasn't what made him a terrible FUC agent.

It was the fact that, if he could go back in time and do it over again, he'd do everything exactly the same. He would still hide Matthew. Still let him recover, still bring him food, still invite the man to his house to talk.

That made him a shitty agent.

Matthew looked like he wanted to say something in reply, but he didn't. He turned and kept moving instead. "Stay close."

"Are there traps or something?" The deeper in they went, the farther away some of the voices seemed. TJ checked his phone. This far down, there was definitely no signal. Luckily, he'd signed in exactly where they would be and for how long. No one was going to lose track of them.

"There shouldn't be, but I didn't know Father would use the gasoline barrels to burn my home without telling me either."

Fair point.

This far down, there had been less debris cleaned away.

Many of the burned doors were still hanging off their hinges. There were some signs taped beside those walls, indicating what had been searched, what was to be followed up on, and what was clear.

Matthew brought him to the lab room. The sign on the door, coded in yellow, showed that follow-up was needed.

"This is the lab." What remained of the door was off its hinges entirely and leaning against the wall.

"They found no bodies?"

"Only the ones we knew about," Matthew said.

Meaning Bobby and the goons who had been left behind.

TJ stepped inside and nearly had the breath sucked out of him.

Christ, this brought back memories.

The room was filled with tanks—what was left of them —all lined against the wall. The glass had shattered from the fire and been swept up by someone, but TJ could never forget what those tanks looked like when they were full.

Large enough to house a person, but barely. Able to contain water for the aquatic shifters like himself or have wood chips and a blanket for the others.

As if they were fucking animals or something.

He shuddered.

"I'm sorry," Matthew said. "You can go if you like."

"I can stay."

"No, I should not have asked you to come. I insisted—"

"I said I can do it." He pulled out his phone, tried to make light of the situation. "Anything's better than those goddamn expense reports for staplers or whatever."

He approached the tanks, his heart thudding as he got close. He kept blinking and seeing flashes of himself in one of those tanks. Sometimes submerged in water, other times not. Waking up one day to the feeling of his entire face hurting, especially around his mouth.

Then seeing his reflection for the first time in the glass.

He'd thought he saw a monster.

For some twisted reason, he had the urge to hop onto the platform and sit down in the tank, just to see if it felt the same.

He decided against it.

"So, what do they think you're gonna find?"

"Not sure," Matthew said, sliding his hand over the dust of a lab table. "Sam is sometimes down here with me or Steve or another of the agents. Someone to keep an eye on me. They'll likely be around soon, but I think they assume I know more than what I do."

"Or that you'll lead them to a secret bunker your dad used?" TJ said it as a joke.

Matthew looked at him as though that wasn't too far off from what was expected. "Maybe."

"Oh, well, I guess if your dad left in a hurry there had to be something he missed."

"Something he might want to come back for," Matthew said. "If we could find what that thing is, it might lure him out. Or give insight to prevent this sort of thing from happening again."

Yeah, everyone had their reasons for wanting to experiment on other people.

Or, in TJ's case, choosing to be experimented on.

"Were you ever in this room?"

Matthew shook his head. "Not that I can recall, no, but the agents are having me comb through them, one by one, after most things of interest are removed. If only to see if that will jog a memory. Maybe trigger some hidden knowledge of a secret door or something."

Made sense.

"Okay, let's keep looking around."

As expected, there were no papers left behind. Not in this room, at least. Any remains of a computer that might've survived was long gone. TJ opened a few drawers and saw what he figured were shattered Bunsen burners.

Matthew looked over the tanks. He seemed a little far away, but he didn't smell stressed or nervous anymore.

"How long does it take for you to sweep a room?"

"Only a few minutes," Matthew said, facing him suddenly, as though coming out of a daze.

"All right, you want to move on? Or wait for Sam or whoever to come down and tell us where else we should go?"

Matthew barely needed to think about it. "I want to move on. See what else is down here."

TJ nodded. He made a note in his phone of the broken Bunsen burners and where he found them. Maybe something survived on the broken glass that could be tested.

TJ wasn't sure if it was necessary, but he signed his initials on the paper next to the busted door to show they'd swept it. Matthew did the same.

He was glad to leave that room, if he was honest.

Matthew led him down the hall. The next two doors were completely blocked off with debris. The floor above them had fallen, blocking off entry.

And escape.

"Thank you for coming," Matthew said suddenly, sounding strangely uncertain. "I appreciate it."

It was that careful, bashful note to his voice that had TJ standing a little straighter. Reminded of their kissing and how he still wasn't sure what it meant for them.

"Yeah, any time," TJ said. "I think it was good for me to come here. To see the tanks."

"Even if they were never yours?"

TJ nodded. "Yeah. I hope no one was ever put into them."

Matthew nodded. "Me as well."

He reached out as though to grab TJ's shoulder and... do what? TJ wasn't sure, and he didn't get to find out. Matthew pulled back and continued to lead the way down the hall.

They followed the lights as far as they went and even a little beyond until they reached another lab. This one had no sign next to the door.

The room hadn't been swept yet. Much farther down the hall, there were warning signs from FUC. Print-offs to not go deeper into this space.

"They say to not go down there," Matthew said. "The floor is unstable beyond this point."

TJ looked at him suddenly, a wide grin catching him. "Yeah, they do say that."

Matthew seemed proud to have been able to read them. TJ didn't dwell on it. He was proud, too, but he knew better than to make a thing out of it. Matthew clearly loved that he was improving his reading skills, but he didn't like being patronized about it.

TJ clapped his shoulder and let that be that, bathing in his pride as though it were his own achievement and not Matthew's.

"Let's just take some pictures of this room then. We won't touch anything or go farther."

It seemed like a good idea. The smell of gas was getting a little thick in here as well anyway, so TJ figured it was near time to head back up.

Mathew gently eased the door open.

No lights. TJ used his phone light, the pair of them staying in the doorway. Not entering. Neither wanting to disturb potential evidence or step through a weak spot in the floor.

They looked in on another lab. Made sense. Most similar rooms were kept on the same floors. The weird thing about this one? It held baby cribs.

That was what they were, though TJ couldn't tell at first. They were so burned he thought they might be the remains of small cages.

Except they weren't.

He found himself entering the space without thinking, moving closer, seeing that the cages were really the remains of the wooden bars of a crib that had collapsed in on itself. The legs had burned away, and some of the bars were little more than ash, but it was clear what the thing had been.

Horror gripped him. He started to back out, bumping into Matthew's chest instead. "Fuck, there might've been little kids here."

Matthew said nothing. He gripped TJ by the shoulders, gently pushing him to the side, getting close to the remains of the crib.

Next to it was a melted car seat then another crib.

Flashes of the pink tanks struck TJ again and again like he was being slapped. He'd tried not to allow himself to think about the fetus-looking thing inside of one, but now he couldn't push it out of his mind.

Were these for children who had been taken? Or for the ones Bazyli had been *growing*?

Matthew reached out, his hand trembling.

TJ grabbed his wrist.

"No, don't touch." Fuck, they shouldn't even be in this room. "We have to get out of here."

"They said there were no other bodies found." Matthew sounded numb, trapped in his thoughts. "Where could this... I've seen these before."

"Maybe they were yours and Rachel's?" It was a long-shot. TJ didn't think they were related, but in case they actually were the fox shifter's children, these could have belonged to them when they were young.

"Maybe this was a storage room for all your baby things?"

Matthew didn't seem so sure. "Maybe. We should go before we—"

Matthew stopped, a heavy groan sounding beneath their feet.

Ice frosted up TJ's spine. He looked at Matthew, and Matthew stared back at him as the floor beneath them crumbled away. The tables, cribs, concrete, and piping crashing around them as they fell deeper into the pit.

9

The crash was loud—loud enough it hurt Matthew's ears—and painful when he landed. The crunching of metal and the crumbling of concrete terrified him like nothing else, but the sound of TJ's shout made his body react, instinct taking over.

He shifted, taking on his oversized owl shape. The debris made it impossible to fly out, and he couldn't see TJ to grab him.

He couldn't see anything!

Matthew shrieked a bird call. His wings flapped, catching on broken rebar and sharp corners, tearing some feathers out.

Danger. Predators nearby. Protect.

Someone yelled at him. To him? He couldn't think. Must escape.

He shrieked again. *Dust everywhere.* He pulled back his massive wings and desperately tried to clear the air, but his flapping only pulled out more feathers and kicked up more dust.

He should be able to see. He was an owl! He could see in the dark! That he couldn't paralyzed him.

"Matthew!"

The second shout made it through. He heard it that time. Matthew blinked, his human mind coming back to the forefront.

TJ was down here with him. He was alive, apparently. Matthew needed to take control of his owl and get them out.

First things first. He shifted back.

"TJ?" he asked, desperate to hear his voice again. He needed to listen more carefully. TJ could be hurt. He could be impaled and dying, and Matthew wouldn't even know it.

"I'm here. Fuck." He sounded in pain.

Matthew smelled blood.

The panic from claustrophobia returned. He'd never wanted to come down here. He'd done it because FUC asked, but each time he'd returned the feeling of dread had gotten worse. He thought bringing TJ with him would help, but now this happened.

"Where are you? Tell me where you are."

He couldn't see. He couldn't fucking see!

Then, a light. Barely.

A soft glow in the distance, through the dust and between part of the ceiling—the floor?—that had collapsed onto them.

"TJ!" Matthew rushed in that direction, still blind from the dust. A piece of broken-off rebar sliced at his thigh like a knife.

He ignored it. The closer he got, the better he could see.

The easier it was to think.

TJ was stuck beneath a piece of the ceiling. There was some blood on the side of his forehead. Looked like a scrape. Nothing that gushed. Thank God.

Matthew didn't know what to do. "Can you move at all?"

TJ shifted his weight beneath the concrete slab. He grimaced. "I think this thing is crushing my foot."

Ice slid down Matthew's back.

TJ looked at him, the soft bulb at the middle of his forehead glowing stronger. Despite the blood and sweat, he managed something close to a smile.

"You're naked."

Oh, he was.

"I shifted."

"Useful for getting out of here." TJ grimaced again. "Help me get this thing off."

Matthew wasn't sure he was strong enough. He was muscular, but this had to weigh so much, and was it right to move it? What if it was holding up other debris that could crush TJ if moved?

"Matt, please."

TJ rarely called him that. He always tried to stay formal, distant. Using the shortened version of his name meant TJ was scared.

Fuck.

"All right. You have to help me, though."

"I'll do what I can."

Matthew felt around the slab, searching for where the most weight was distributed without putting pressure on it.

"Hurry," TJ said, clearly trying to keep it together.

Matthew found a few more big rocks the stone had landed on. It was enough to stop the slab from crushing TJ's lower body entirely but not enough to save him from getting pinned.

"Okay. I think I can lift it on this side, and when I do, you're going to have to drag yourself backward. Can you do it?"

"Arms are working. Do it."

"All right." Matthew got into position, putting his hand under the slab, praying nothing else broke apart or that he wasn't making a horrible mistake.

"One, two…"

Matthew lifted.

Even just lifting the corner of the thing took all his strength. His thighs trembled. He barely pulled the concrete block up a few centimeters. Felt like nothing at all and his entire body burned from the effort.

"Go, go, go!" he gritted out, distantly aware of TJ pulling himself backward, away from the rock that had him pinned.

The scent of blood got thicker in the air as TJ scrambled away from the rock.

Matthew felt like his arms were about to pop out of their sockets.

He was sorry. He was so sorry, but he couldn't hold it up anymore. With numb fingers, his strength gave out. The slab fell back, much farther than Matthew thought he'd lifted it, cracking the stone and debris beneath it into nothing.

Oh God.

"TJ?" He wobbled around the slab, trying to see with that light on TJ's forehead.

"I'm all right. I'm out." TJ exhaled, his body covered in dust, his leg bleeding. "I think I broke my leg."

No.

Matthew jumped over the slab. He could barely make out the length of TJ's body, but at least he could see it. He didn't have to worry about jostling something that could fall on him.

His hands immediately went for TJ's face, gently holding him, looking for… what? Rachel knew more about health and first aid than he did. He wasn't smart enough for any of this. Wasn't he not supposed to move TJ at all? Was he supposed to worry about TJ's neck?

Too late for all of that.

TJ stared at him, that light getting brighter. "H-hey, you good?"

Matthew blinked. He was still holding TJ's dusty cheek and jaw. "I..."

"You're shaking. We're okay," TJ said. His hands slid up and down Matthew's shoulders and arms, like he was comforting a terrified animal. "We're good."

How was TJ the one comforting him? It should be the other way around. Matthew wanted to leap into action, to confidently tell TJ they were getting out of there. He wanted to throw the man onto his back, shift into his owl form, and fly them out of this pit.

But he still couldn't move. Frozen, kneeling impotently in front of TJ in this fucking gasoline-smelling pit that kept trying to kill them.

"I... I shouldn't've brought you... I shouldn't've..."

"Hey, hey." TJ gripped him from behind the neck. That caught Matthew's attention. "I'm all right, and so are you. Listen, you hear that?"

He didn't. It must have showed on his face.

"Come on. You're an owl. I *know* your hearing's better than mine," TJ said, his grin looking more like a painful flinch. "Listen. Close your eyes."

Matthew didn't want to close his eyes. He didn't want to be trapped in the dark, but TJ's calm, easy voice commanded obedience from the wild animal inside his head, so he closed his eyes and listened to the sound of TJ's strong, calm heart, and in turn, that eased his own.

Then, he did hear them.

Voices, in the distance above them, echoing. FUC agents were everywhere. He and TJ weren't alone down here.

"Are you sure they'll get us out?" A small part of Matthew still didn't fully trust them. He realized that now. His father's teachings, his *warnings*, were still with him, it seemed. "What if they leave us down here?"

"I promise, they won't, and if they do—" TJ hissed suddenly.

His leg looked so busted up. So horrible. Matthew wished he could take the pain from him. Wished he was the wounded one instead.

"If they do, we got you to fly us out of here."

Matthew didn't want to admit that his wings could stretch wider than the gaping hole above them. Not to mention the rest of the hanging debris. Getting out of here on his own would be tricky, but he figured he could pull it off without electrocuting himself.

With another person? Someone injured clinging to his back feathers?

"Well, I'm glad you have faith in them. I won't leave here until they can get you out."

"No, go."

Matthew jerked back. "What?"

TJ nodded to the dark hole above them. "I have no idea how many floors we fell, but you can't be down here. The sooner they know where we are, the sooner I can sit my ass in a hospital bed with pay for a few days. Go on."

"I won't leave you." Matthew was insulted TJ thought he would. Flying away while TJ was stuck down there, injured and in pain, shot something into him that made him forget his fear of this dark pit.

"Matt." TJ's voice, in pain, was also firm. "I want to get out of here. I've got my built-in headlamp," He pointed to the soft bulb at his forehead. "You can go, and I'll be fine. Tell them where I am, and I can wait."

The plan was a good one. Matthew hated it for that reason. He didn't want to leave TJ here, but it was true. The sooner the FUC agents knew where they were, the better this would be for TJ because he would get out sooner.

Still, the sheer amount of trust TJ had in his voice, the certainty that Matthew would return for him, made his heart swell. A week ago Matthew had been so furious with TJ's supposed betrayal that he was ready to never speak to him again. Now, here TJ was, injured and in pain, and telling Matthew to leave him behind.

He did not deserve the man's affections.

Matthew kissed him. He held TJ's face in his hands and kissed him because his heart hurt so much he couldn't stand it.

TJ seemed surprised but not completely thrown off. Matthew was pretty sure the guy was also smiling through it.

It wasn't a great kiss, if Matthew was honest. They were both sweaty and a little bloody, the air down here was stale, and if Matthew could taste the dust on TJ's lips, then he knew TJ could taste the grime on his.

Still felt nice, though. Still felt a little like a promise.

"I'll come back for you," Matthew said, immediately after pulling back, still holding TJ's face.

TJ nodded.

"Don't try to move." Matthew pointed down at him, rising to his feet. He had no idea where their phones were, but he wouldn't need them. This wouldn't take long. "Keep your light on. I'll come back down the instant I tell them where you are."

This place terrified him, but leaving TJ alone in it terrified him more.

"O-Okay." TJ blinked, looking a little dazed. Maybe from the kiss, or the certainty in Matthew's voice, or the pain in his leg. Matthew couldn't be sure.

"All right. Wait here." Matthew immediately felt dumb. Where else was TJ going to go?

Matthew shifted quickly. The dust had settled some more, and with TJ's light, his vision was much better than it had been a few moments ago.

He had a mission now as well.

He spread his wings, hearing the voices of more FUC agents above them.

Jesus, they hadn't just fallen through one or two floors. They were at least another five floors down.

He shivered. TJ was lucky he wasn't dead.

Matthew searched for his way up, a path that would avoid hanging, tangled wires, as well as any other debris he could accidentally let tumble onto TJ if his talons or the tips of his wings so much as touched them.

He made his path, spread his wings, and pushed himself into the air.

10

TJ wanted to pretend everything was all fine and swell when he sent Matthew up that dark, imposing-looking shaft, but he felt like absolute shit.

He hated being alone down here. Hated it more when he was alone because, holy fuck, it was hot, he was dirty and sweaty, and his leg felt like it was going to fall off.

Matthew told him to keep the light on, but at a certain point, he needed a break. He shut down the light just for a little while. He needed to rest, to focus more of his energy on his leg.

Fuck, it hurt so badly.

It felt like an eternity before lights shone down on him, brighter than anything he could have produced.

The light was almost blinding.

Agents in all kinds of gear slid down ropes, their own battery-operated headlamps making the space even brighter.

Where was Matthew?

He wasn't among them. TJ panicked. Something must have happened. He said he'd come back.

Someone rushed to him, getting to his knees. Smelled like a wolf.

"Warren?" TJ recognized him.

"Hey, yeah. We're here. Hold still."

Two more agents rushed forward. Paramedics. TJ found himself poked and prodded. A neck brace was clipped around his throat, and lights were flashed into his eyes.

He turned away from the light. "My eyes are fine. So's my neck." He didn't mean to sound like a baby about it, but fuck his leg was throbbing. It felt swollen and hot, and he'd almost let them cut it off right now if it meant he didn't have to feel this pain.

"We're not taking a risk. We have to pull you up with a gurney and a pulley."

Then TJ yowled as one of the paramedics stabbed him with a needle in his thigh.

Then he decided he liked the guy when his leg felt numb and didn't hurt anymore.

"Where's Matt?" TJ asked, gasping in relief.

"He wanted to come down, but Sam pulled rank."

"What? Why?"

"He's too big, and we can't have him getting in the way when you're injured like this."

TJ frowned. He didn't get it. That wasn't any rule he'd heard of. He couldn't imagine someone telling Miranda Brownsmith that her saber-toothed bunny was too big to help on a mission.

The only real reason agents were held back was when there was a conflict of interest. A mate or some sort of relationship.

Did FUC know?

TJ felt himself tensing up.

Warren leveled him with a very even stare.

Fuck, of course they did. Matt rushed up there, naked in a panic. Did he try a little too hard to get back down here? Did his actions give something away?

"He's still up there. He's getting some spare clothes, and he's waiting for you. So let's just pull you out of here before he turns back into that giant owl and scares the new guys."

TJ was one of those new guys, and he didn't think Matt's transformation was scary. More impressive, really.

"Okay, let's go." He was eager to get out of here. He was over this whole fucking room, and it was embarrassing that he'd been brought in to help just to get injured and need an evacuation.

On the way out of the oversized space, with all the lights flashing and the dust settled, he got a look at what was around him. Along the walls, some smashed under debris, others still intact, were more tanks.

They were smaller than the ones above. More cylindrical.

Inside them was a red-looking liquid.

And small creatures. Animals floating dead within.

He hoped they were animals.

MATTHEW WAS THERE when TJ was pulled out, wearing a pair of sweatpants and a spare lab coat, though his feet were bare.

The guy looked absolutely wrecked.

A selfish little part of TJ was glad to see Matthew was worried, that he'd stayed, but the other part of TJ was glad to be pulled out in one piece so he could put Matthew's fears at ease.

He wished he wasn't wrapped up and as stiff as he was,

but the fresh air sure felt good. It felt even better when Matthew hopped into the ambulance with him and grabbed his hand. No one tried to kick Matthew out either. That was nice.

By then, TJ was feeling more than a little groggy, maybe a touch loopy, but that could be the result of that awesome drug he was injected with that had taken away the pain.

TJ held Matt's hand as tight as he could until he passed out, the hum of the engine lulling him.

When he woke up, his hand was cold and empty. Matthew was gone, and TJ was lying in a hospital bed.

He groaned. This was too familiar.

Diane walked in barely a moment after he opened his eyes. She had a clipboard in hand, paused in the doorway at the sight of him, and smiled. "That was good timing."

"Nice to see you, too."

Back in his early days at FUCN'A, this woman had applied creams to his mouth, had stitched his wounds, and held him when he cried like a little kid in her arms when his deformity got the better of him.

He didn't like being here, but a little part of him was happy to see her.

"Where's—"

"I sent your mate home. He needed a shower, badly, and some food. That was a few hours ago, so he'll probably be back soon."

"We're not... That wasn't..." They kissed a couple of times. That didn't make them mates.

"Ah, my mistake." Diane tilted her head to the side a bit. She seemed to consider something. "He refused to leave your side. Even threatened a few of the nursing staff to make sure you were treated well."

Jesus Christ. The warm fuzzies hit him while he thought

about Matthew getting all possessive and protective over him when he was down for the count.

Diane had a little smirk on her face. "It seemed like the sort of behavior I'd seen before, but maybe you're just good friends."

They were a good something. A few kisses didn't make a relationship though, and it definitely wasn't something TJ wanted to talk to anyone about. Not even Diane.

"Your leg had multiple fractures," Diane said, changing the subject. "The bone was sticking out right about here"—she gently tapped his cast with her pen, and he didn't feel it.—"and I'll bet you're glad you were unconscious while we put you back together."

"Definitely." He shivered.

"Luckily it was nothing above the knee. If you really want, you could even walk with this cast, but I don't recommend doing too much of that today."

"Great. When can I get out of here?"

"Well, not that we're in a huge need of the bed, but it's a broken leg. With shifter healing and the work we already did, you'll be back on your feet within the week, but I don't want to hear about any hard exercise for at least two weeks." She made a show of lifting a page on her clipboard, pretending to read it, then dropping it down with a smile. "You can head home today if you like."

A soft knock sounded. TJ's heart did a weird pitter-patter thing when Matthew appeared.

He looked freshly showered, clean-shaven, and he actually had flowers—fucking *flowers*—in his hand. "Sorry, I didn't know he was with his doctor. I'll be right outside."

"No." TJ sat up quickly, as if to follow Matthew out the door.

Diane didn't react. She appeared to be reading her notes again, though the corner of her mouth lifted just slightly.

God, his face felt so hot. Had to be another side effect from the drugs. "You don't have to go. I was just getting an update."

"He'll be discharged soon," Diane added. "We'll just go over any medications he needs and exercise he can do, and then you can take him home. You're right on time."

"Oh." Matthew nodded, looking at the white daisies and peach-colored roses. Then he looked at TJ. "That's good."

"Yes, very. He's lucky you were there with him," Diane said. She suddenly clicked her pen. "Nolan spoke to you already?"

"Yes, ma'am." Matthew nodded politely. "Gave another sample. He said he'd get back to me when he could."

TJ frowned. Another sample? Were they testing him for something? Matt didn't look sick.

Whatever. TJ was in too much of a good mood to think of anything else. It was definitely embarrassing to have Matt standing there with flowers after Diane thought they were mates.

But he liked it.

It was stupid and gooey, but TJ actually liked it.

They might not be mates, but guys who were friends didn't give each other flowers.

Even if they were really good friends.

Guys who were friends didn't kiss each other, either.

So, yeah, maybe they were something more than just friends.

Diane went over TJ's prescriptions. She gave him a checklist of the movements and exercises he was allowed to do in his current state. He was not allowed to lift anything heavier than ten pounds, and she even handed over her personal number in case he had questions or concerns.

Thanks to the healing, she expected him to be out of the cast in just a few days. More or less, it was only there because she wanted to be more safe than sorry, considering how many breaks his tibia and fibula had. It was important to keep everything in place, so his shifter healing didn't knit anything back together at any odd angles.

He was also not to call after ten at night unless it was a huge emergency.

FUC doctors didn't mess around, it seemed.

Matthew wheeled him out of the building and toward TJ's truck, and that was that.

"I'm sorry. I hope you don't mind I was driving it," Matthew said. "I'll pay you back the gas when I can."

As if TJ was even worried about that. "You still staying at the apartment?"

"Yes, though I let Rachel know about your injury. She, ah, recommended I buy you the flowers. She sends her love."

Matthew helped him into the truck.

"I guess she's not so mad at me anymore?"

Matthew barely held his gaze. "I talked to her. She understands your position now. And mine."

Matthew's hands were strong and firm on TJ's waist as he pulled him into the truck. Then gentle and smooth as he helped TJ lift his busted leg into the foot well.

It fucking hurt, but he barely noticed the pain. All kinds of warmth were hitting him. TJ wet his lips.

"You should stay at my place tonight."

Matt froze. Stared at him. "Your place?" He sounded hopeful.

Right, after all the kissing, there was only one thing it

could mean to ask him to spend the night. But maybe Matt didn't understand that. TJ shrugged, nervous.

"We could order takeout. Watch a movie."

"I could assist you around the house."

TJ swallowed hard. "Yeah, that too."

They could do more of that amazing kissing. TJ ached to put his mouth over Matt's. He wanted to kiss him again and see if the rush of heat was still the same.

Who was he kidding? It probably was.

In a bold show of confidence, Matt put one hand on the doorframe of the truck, the other on the door itself. He leaned in close, eyes flashing, looking like a bird that was about to eat well tonight.

"You gotta know what I want to do to you."

Christ, TJ never heard his voice sound like... like *that* before.

"All good things, I hope." TJ tried to joke it off. Truthfully, he was a little nervous. A little out of breath.

A little of a lot of things.

Matt tapped his finger on the doorframe of the vehicle. He seemed to be contemplating something.

Then he made a decision.

Both large, calloused hands found the back of TJ's neck. He pulled TJ close, and TJ leaned forward.

The feel of his mouth on TJ's was like none of the previous kisses they'd shared. Not the first one, which was all fumbling, fearful, and unsure for both of them. Not the second one, which felt more like forgiveness.

No, this one made TJ shiver from top to bottom. A shot of warmth and pleasure hit him in the gut. He grabbed Matt around the neck, trying to get closer, to pull him in deeper.

He would have if it weren't for his stupid leg.

This kiss felt like what came before sex.

TJ was eager to get to that part. The sex part. He wanted Matt with his clothes off.

He wanted Matt's dick in his mouth.

"Holy shit," TJ said, blinking, dazed when Matt pulled back for a breath.

Matt stared at him, so close they could be kissing again. He looked pleased and a little innocent, and maybe a little like he was searching for TJ's approval.

"That was... real damn nice."

"I'm glad." Matt's shoulders sagged, like he really was relieved to hear it. His mouth cracked into a wide grin. "I'm so fucking glad."

He kissed TJ again.

Good. TJ wanted more.

Were they supposed to be driving somewhere? Fuck, yeah, his house.

He'd let Matt fool around with him in the truck if he could get away with it, but even his shifter healing wouldn't have him ready to get screwed in the cab. He knew that much.

Now he was hard. Fuck, his stupid dick liked the idea of that, getting hot and heavy in there. Seeing what positions they could get into.

"Fuck, hurry up and get into the driver's side please." TJ forced himself to inch back, out of Matt's arms. The fact that his pants were too tight and his cock throbbed while they were in the parking lot was definitely not okay with him.

Matt didn't seem to mind. He grinned.

TJ growled at him, his face getting uncomfortably hot. "What?"

"Nothing. I think I like seeing you like this."

The heat got worse, but the embarrassment that hit him suddenly felt... good?

TJ stared at his hands in his lap. "Yeah, yeah. Don't let it go to your head. Let's just go before I change my mind."

"You won't do that," Matt said, sounding a little too confidant with himself, walking a little too tall toward the driver's side, and still grinning like his prize was won as he started the engine.

TJ grinned. Who was he kidding? Whatever hang-ups he had about being seen so... vulnerable in public, Matt was right. The prize was already won.

He just had to get TJ home and naked so he could claim it.

He couldn't drive fast enough.

11

"This...this isn't possible." Albert shook his head, reading the papers. Beverly leaned over, reading next to him and Diane pressed her lips together.

They were all sitting together in her office, chairs huddled close. This didn't seem like the sort of situation where Diane would be behind her desk.

"Are you sure?" Beverly stared at her and then at the papers again.

Each print-off said the same thing.

"How is this possible?

"We're doing the tests again, on a different machine, in a different location, just to be sure," Diane said. "Though, after five tests, I thought you should be aware of what we had."

Five separate tests, three of which were done with different lab technicians. One that had been done with fresh beakers and gloves and literally everything else that needed to be thrown away after use.

Same result.

So now they were sending Matthew's saliva and blood to another FUC lab.

Somewhere Albert and Beverly's son had never been.

"If this is true," Albert said, "what does it mean? I mean I've seen him before; he's a grown man. In his mid-twenties at least."

"And isn't he Rachel's brother? She's the red panda shifter?" Beverly asked.

Diane struggled against the urge to crack her knuckles. An old, nervous habit she'd thought she'd left behind years ago. It suddenly reared itself again.

"FUC agents are still looking into that," Diane said, eyeing Albert. "I'm sure you've noticed you haven't been getting the updates anymore."

"Because of this?" Albert lifted his papers, his expression incredulous. "Because you all think this guy is... that he might be..."

He couldn't finish.

Beverly covered her mouth with her hands.

They both looked like they'd been hit by a truck with this information.

"To be honest, my decision was to keep this from you until the last test was done, but with the discovery of the tanks and the bodies in the compound, it was decided you should know this was a possibility."

Shifters being taken for experimentation was nothing new, but as far as Diane knew, it was usually only done on older victims, not babies. As for possibly cloning? She was still looking into whether this had ever happened at all.

And what it might mean for Albert and Beverly Huntly.

Almost three years ago, while pregnant, Beverly had disappeared. She had been found by her husband out in the woods, in her beaver shape, building a dam. She had no child with her, and couldn't recall her husband or being pregnant.

Her memories had only fully returned when the child was returned to her, safely, thanks to John's guilt. The baby had been examined. Every test that could be done was done. It was decided he was boringly healthy, and the little family had been given a second chance.

A kidnapped infant had been the worst news FUC had faced in a long time, but the baby had been recovered. There needed to be more happy endings in the world, and Beverly's son was just that. He was a healthy little toddler who loved *Paw Patrol*, hated broccoli, and cried when he got his shots like most kids his age did.

"So Bazyli was cloning the girl," Albert said. "You all know this for sure?"

"Based on what we found in those tanks? Yes." Diane sighed, her stomach turning at the thought.

"Why?"

"We don't know why, but we have some guesses." She shook her head. "Apparently Rachel has no idea." For the moment, FUC intended on keeping it that way.

"And your tests are saying that this... *man* is genetically identical to our boy?" Beverly asked, her face horrified. "A... clone?" She whispered the last word.

"How can he be?" Albert asked. "That's a grown man."

"Who shifts into a saber-toothed owl. A large one," Diane reminded. She reached for her coffee mug, but she didn't drink from it. She just wanted something to hold before she started popping her knuckles again. "To be honest, that alone had me wondering if he was related to you. An over-sized animal is rare. Your beaver shape is already oversized."

The size of a small bear.

"But it's possible. Miranda's rabbit shape is huge," Beverly said.

"Yes, that's true, and if he were a rabbit, we might have wondered if he belonged somewhere on Miranda's family tree for him. But a horned owl shifter? There's not many of them around. And he does look a little like Albert."

Albert had said nothing for a moment. His cheeks were noticeably pale.

"We're checking it again," Diane assured them. They had already been through so much. They didn't need this. Hell, no one needed to hear news like this.

"We do have to deal with the fact that we don't know what was done to your son when he was taken from you. Mother had him for weeks before John returned him. He was in one piece, but that's long enough that they could've harvested all the DNA they needed to create a clone."

Aging the clone, however? That was beyond her pay grade.

Of all the things that had been done to humans and shifters alike, of all the things that were possible, this seemed... impossible It shouldn't be real. But what other explanation was there?

"What did he say?" Albert asked. "Matthew? Does he know?"

She shook her head. "We haven't told him anything. He's been fully cooperating and doesn't seem to think anything strange is going on. I suppose he doesn't realize it's out of the ordinary for us to ask him to return so many times to give more samples."

"Where is he now?"

That was a whole other thing she needed to get into with them. "He's volunteered to take care of TJ. They were at the compound when it collapsed. TJ has a break, but it should be fine in a while."

"Right. They're friends?" Beverly asked.

"Seems that way." Probably more than that, if Diane was right, but it didn't seem right for her to tell all of Matthew's business. They might not actually be his parents, after all, and he was an adult, not a child. Matthew could make his own decisions on who he wanted to know about what he did.

Then Albert shocked her with the knowledge he had. "Matthew pulled TJ out of the compound before it lit up the first time. TJ was hiding him from FUC for several months after that. Yeah, they're close."

Of course the damned owl shifter, the beak-in-a-book librarian would figure it out without her saying anything.

Diane almost smiled.

"If he is a clone of your son, what will you do?" Diane needed to know that much. Working at the academy with so many rescued experiments meant she'd become more than just their physician. She cared about what happened to her patients. "What would you like us to do to help you?"

Albert and Beverley looked at each other. Then at Diane. She'd never seen them so helpless before.

"Find out for sure first," Albert said. "We shouldn't tell him anything in case there's a mix-up. Not until you're all sure about this."

Diane was pleased with that decision. Beverly also nodded, still appearing dazed as she leaned against her husband's arm.

"I agree," Diane said. "I'll keep you updated on the situation. When we speak to Rachel, there will be FUC counselors present, and we don't want her brother venting to her about the tanks before we have more information."

"Is she a clone of a kidnapped baby, too?" Beverly asked, sitting a little straighter, her cheeks ghostly white against her brown hair.

"We don't think so." Diane looked at Albert. "You've read the notes on Bazyli Smith, I assume?"

"Yes." Albert closed his eyes and leaned back in his chair. He shoved his hand under his glasses and rubbed at his eyes. "The man had a daughter who died. Fuck... that's... Yeah."

"He wanted to bring her back to life." Diane nodded. "That's the theory we're working with for the moment." The cloning theory seemed to make sense, but it brought them back to the aging mystery. If Rachel and Matthew were clones, how were they adult-aged?

They'd confirmed the fox shifter had a daughter. Old photos had been found, birth certificates tracked down. A little red-haired girl. The mother had died in childbirth and the daughter when she was just three years old.

It meant Bazyli wasn't like the previous scientists FUC had dealt with who were crazed or simply full of themselves, wanting to kidnap random shifters and humans for their own experiments.

He wasn't like Mastermind, who hated herself for her small size and wished to change her shape. He wasn't like Mother, who, after losing her own children, wanted to kidnap an entire family for herself. A whole slew of shifters who would agree to her experiments to save them. She'd wished to manipulate those suffering into loving her, and in doing so, she just made them suffer more.

No, Bazyli wanted his own child back, not a replacement, but the real thing.

"Should Rachel have more security?" Albert asked, his mind going where Diane's had.

She nodded. "It's already done. I was told that no one expects Matthew to be contacted, but someone will watch his apartment just in case."

And TJ's as well, since she got the feeling Matthew wouldn't be spending much time at his own place.

12

Matthew had been to TJ's house dozens of times. The last time he hadn't been half as nervous as this.

That first time, though... Starving, dirty, and just looking for... He wasn't sure what. TJ had stopped short at the sight of him, looked around to make sure no one could see them, then promptly dragged Matthew into the house for a shower, a warm meal, and then washed his clothes.

On Matthew's next visit, a newer set of clothes, in his size, were waiting for him. TJ gave him another meal, another brief rest, and then more and more conversation.

With every visit, they grew closer.

But this was definitely the first time TJ held Matthew's hand while he twisted the key and unlocked the door.

Matthew could hear the pulsing of TJ's heart. He wanted to ask if TJ was all right, but TJ was the one gripping Matthew's hand like a lifeline, dragging him into the house, slamming and locking the door again.

Then he didn't move. Matthew didn't either.

Matthew had no idea what to do. The realization felt

sudden and blunt, like that old wrecking ball video he saw all over the Internet.

Finally, thankfully, TJ looked at him.

His eyes were bright.

Matthew smiled, wanting to put him at ease. Wanting to touch and kiss him some more. "You want me to put on a movie?"

"What?" TJ blinked wide.

"A movie?" Matthew never felt as powerful as this. But he knew TJ needed a minute. "We talked about it before coming here?"

"Oh. Oh!" TJ shook his head, like he was coming out of a trance. "Yeah, sorry. I just... yeah."

TJ started to move toward the sitting room. Matthew didn't like that. He wished the clinic had at least given him a set of crutches. "Let me help you."

"It's okay, Diane said I could walk on it."

He could walk on it, but that didn't mean Matthew had to like it.

TJ made it to the couch quickly, not looking at him and grabbing the remote. He flipped on the TV and turned it to Netflix, as if to pick out something for them to watch.

Matthew sighed. He brought the flowers to TJ's kitchen table. The man didn't have a vase lying about or a glass tall enough for their stems, so he set them down gently until one could be purchased, or maybe he could find a bucket somewhere.

"I've got some money now. What do you want to order?" Matthew said instead.

"You don't have to do that."

"I want to." He got the feeling TJ didn't want to be coddled too much, but TJ had taken care of him and fed him for too long. He wanted to be the one to provide the meal this time.

He felt oddly strong about that. Giving TJ food right now, making him comfortable, it wasn't simply returning all the many favors he owed the man. It was something else.

TJ finally looked at him, and he seemed to get it, that Matthew needed to give him something to eat. It was some primal instinct to provide, something he couldn't just shut off.

"All right, uh, I'm in the mood for something simple. Sandwiches or whatever."

"I can do that." Matthew jumped at the chance. "Where can I order it from?"

It felt strange pulling out a phone that was his, on an account that was his own, and searching through the food apps that would deliver this far out.

TJ suggested one of the few restaurants that were in the next town over, and it worked out well. They delivered, and it would be good food, nothing overly fast. Matthew didn't think his stomach could handle anything huge right now, so when TJ requested a club with fries, Matthew ordered the same, adding drinks and a cheesecake to the order for sharing just because he could.

With a few taps on his phone, it was done.

"That was easy."

"Watch out for that," TJ said, grimacing as he eased himself onto the couch. "When I was a kid, I blew through so much of my money like that. It's easy to spend a few hundred dollars and barely notice."

Matthew looked down at his phone. The ease of the transactions could be the most troublesome thing to deal with. He didn't think he was in danger of spending all of what FUC gave him so quickly, but he never wanted to be in that position either. He wanted to earn and save enough to protect and provide for TJ and his sister.

Matthew sat down next to him. "Will you show me how to not spend hundreds of dollars on these?"

"Oh, well, uh…" TJ scratched the back of his neck. "Well, I guess it's all the basic stuff. Eat in whenever you can. Don't buy stuff you don't need."

"No, I mean how do I not spend everything I have on this?" He held up the phone.

Matthew liked having it, but now he was worried.

"Oh, well, let me see what you have. If that's okay…" TJ paused, pulling his hand back before he could take the phone.

"Yes, it's all right." Matthew all but shoved it at him.

TJ looked at it like he wasn't sure what to do with it either. Impossible, since Matthew had seen him on his own phone plenty of times.

"Look, I don't want to insult you…"

Matthew deflated. TJ thought he was unintelligent.

"But lots of people don't like being told how to spend their money or how to budget. I can barely do it."

Relief hit him. This was somewhat familiar territory for them. "I don't mind. You helped me with my reading studies when Rachel couldn't. I know you know I'm not very well educated on these things."

TJ's shoulders went stiff. "I never judged you for that."

"I know," Matthew said, feeling so happy, even though a part of him had worried about that exact thing just a minute ago. "I appreciate you for that, but I won't pretend that I know what I'm doing here either. I want to… I want to have a better chance of a proper life. I can't do that if I spend everything I have. Even though I wouldn't mind spending it all on you."

A small flush of color dusted across TJ's cheeks. Matthew didn't miss the way he glanced to the flowers sitting on his table.

"Yeah, okay. Uh, dude, it's not something to be ashamed of. FUC gave you your first paycheck. Lots of people play around with their firsts."

"Because most of them are still teenagers with minimal responsibilities." Matthew was not a teenager, and he had plans to achieve and shit to do. He wanted to know what he should be doing here.

"Right. I'm just saying lots of people buy more than they're supposed to. If you're worried about accidentally spending too much at the beginning, I guess I wouldn't get a credit card right away. When you do, make sure the limit is low enough that you can pay off the whole thing in one or two shots."

Matthew nodded, leaning close, paying special attention as TJ did his best to teach him financial responsibility.

TJ seemed more embarrassed by the topic than Matthew did. He even made sure to remind Matthew every other sentence that he was not an expert and that his ways were not the only ways.

Matthew opened his new banking app, and TJ seemed shocked with the ease Matthew had in showing him his accounts. There was a thousand dollars in his checking account after the purchase of the flowers and the meal. Matthew felt a little rich, until TJ started getting into savings accounts and retirement plans, emergency funds, and other expenses—including taking over his rent once the first month FUC provided was over.

It was an educational discussion. Netflix was entirely forgotten about as Matthew listened to his instructor, the pair of them leaning together over the phone, their heads touching.

"I know it's a lot," TJ said, snorting a short laugh. "And lots of the advice I gave you is stuff I'm not even doing yet, so don't stress too much about it."

TJ looked at him, and Matthew looked back.

They were so close. TJ's body was warm.

A swell of affection hit him in the chest. "Thank you for teaching me this."

Thank you for not judging me. For not thinking I'm dumb.

"Yeah, anytime." TJ handed the phone back. "You should probably talk to a financial advisor as some point. To make sure I don't screw you over with my dumb advice." He said it with a soft laugh. He looked so damn handsome in that moment that Matthew couldn't help but kiss him.

TJ inhaled a shocked gasp. Matthew just knew what he was supposed to do with that, so he went for it, leaning forward, his hands on TJ's neck and face, his tongue gently pushing between TJ's parted lips to taste inside.

It was better than he thought possible. Matthew moaned. So did TJ. Matthew had to pull back from it when his dick suddenly pulsed a little too hard.

He was out of breath.

Thank God TJ was as well.

The doorbell rang.

Matthew jumped up. He'd forgotten food was coming. At least now he could feed TJ.

The delivery man gave him the paper bag and his receipt, and when the door was safely shut and locked again, Matthew felt a little more himself. His stupid cock was still aching but not tenting noticeably anymore.

When he turned around, TJ was right there.

Chest to chest, in his personal space, as it was called.

How he'd gotten up and hobbled his way over with the cast on and not be heard, Matthew had no idea.

"Are you—"

"Yes, give me that." He took the paper bag out of Matthew's hands, bent down, and set it on the floor where it did not belong, standing straight once more.

Matthew had no idea what to expect, but he liked it very much when TJ kissed him this time, an arm lazily curling around Matthew's neck and shoulders, the other around his middle.

It felt right to let his hands settle on TJ's narrow waist. The man leaned against him a bit. Matthew wanted to steady him. Didn't want to make it harder for him than needed with that leg.

Finally, Matthew felt it again. That instinct he got back at the hospital when he told TJ what he wanted to do to him.

It didn't matter that he had no clue what he was doing, that he'd never done it before with anyone. This was right. This was going to happen.

Matthew walked TJ back just two steps before TJ hissed, gripping his shoulders tighter.

He didn't sound in pain, more that he'd almost lost his balance.

"Fuck, sorry."

"No, it's me," Matthew said.

More of that not thinking took over as he bent forward, neatly scooping TJ into his arms.

TJ made that shocked sound again. "What the—? Are you serious?"

"Yes."

Matthew could deal with TJ's embarrassment later. It was imperative that he got the man horizontal.

"I wish my stupid leg would feel faster," TJ grouched, though he seemed in a good mood when Matthew set him down on his unmade bed.

That reminded Matt of something. "Shifters usually heal pretty fast."

"I'm not a real shifter," TJ said. "Had the juices pumped into me in a lab. I heal faster, but I can't just change and have my bones right themselves."

That was a shame, but at least he had some quick healing going for him.

Except TJ pursed his lips and refused to look at Matthew again.

Matthew thought he understood.

"It doesn't bother me that you were made into a shifter."

"I know." TJ shrugged, like he didn't entirely believe it. "It just bothers some people."

"Not me." Matthew grabbed his chin, kissing his mouth.

God, he would never get tired of that taste. He hoped TJ always tasted like this.

The soft glow at the center of TJ's forehead gently brightened.

Matthew grinned through his kiss. "That's cute."

"Yeah, well..." TJ rubbed the light away. "It's the only part of me that you could call cute. My animal shape is fucking ugly."

There was no getting around that. Matthew had looked up what that fish looked like. He'd seen what TJ had been before FUC had been able to fix him.

"I like to think of it as being fierce."

TJ snorted, grinning. "You don't have to sweet-talk me so much. You've got me in bed already."

"I'm not sweet-talking anything," Matthew said, even though he actually had been doing just that. "I like how you look. This face"—he slid his thumb across TJ's jaw, hesitating over his lower lip—"and your animal shape. I love knowing you can inspire fear in the hearts of your enemies."

TJ actually laughed. Matthew preened.

That was the reaction he wanted.

"You're such an—"

Matthew kissed him again, silencing him before he could say it.

Yes. For some reason, when it came to this guy, Matthew was a complete idiot.

———

BAZYLI'D HAD no intention of coming back. It was too dangerous, but there was no other option. He had no one to turn to. No other labs to pull resources from.

No choice but to slink around in the shrubs like a thieving fox.

He needed another specimen.

His little girl...

He'd left in too much of a hurry. There'd not been enough power to sustain the tank. No matter. A transfusion. That was what his latest Rachel needed.

Except...

He stopped short, growling low in his throat. The compound was still surrounded by FUC agents. Their vehicles. Their little encampments and lights. They'd brought machines and equipment and had boots on the ground.

They were still here. He should have known.

He slunk along the tree line. His paws were light and quick, as they always were. Not a leaf crunched and no twigs snapped. He was quick, but there were shifters who could hear the slightest disturbance. Bears, wolves, moose... was that even a panda shifter he scented? No matter. They wouldn't be smelling him.

Thankfully, the wind was with him. All he had to worry about were the birds in the sky. He wasn't entirely sure if they were real birds or scouts. He wouldn't take the risk of being spotted from above.

But he couldn't get in.

Baz inwardly cursed.

Every entrance, even the secret ones, were surrounded by agents of FUC. Worse, they pulled his equipment from the wreckage.

When he burned the compound, there should have still been rooms safe from the fire, but it looked like FUC had found them.

He saw the tanks. Men and women in white lab coats were categorizing everything. The pink liquid in test tubes they put under microscopes in their makeshift labs, the broken glass...

He didn't know where the little bodies from the tanks were. They could not have survived outside of their tanks. Perhaps FUC had already taken them back headquarters.

Baz dug his claws into the dirt. He growled low and angry.

A man in the distance snapped his head up. He must have especially excellent hearing to have picked that up.

No matter. Baz turned tail and rushed through the forest.

Fuck. *FUCK*.

He needed those tanks. He needed those specimens. They were dead anyway, unsustainable outside their tanks, but their blood would have been useful.

Rachel Four.

No. He *couldn't*.

She lived though, and hers was the closest match. The only one to survive outside the tanks.

She could be useful.

Baz slowed to a trot. He kept moving, acid churning in his belly, but it was too dangerous to stop now. He needed to get back to his car and then return to his new lodgings.

He had no other choice.

She called him Daddy. Had smiled at him and trusted him.

His daughter, his real one, would die without her.

FUC would be watching Rachel Four. No doubt they hoped he would attempt to make contact.

Baz walked two hours back to his vehicle. He shifted, dressed, and pulled up his notes from his computer. He checked the data on the tank back home.

Still alive. Barely.

He punched his steering wheel.

Then hit it again and again, until his fist and fingers throbbed hotly.

How did they find those rooms?

Perhaps Matthew...?

Regardless, FUC was relentless. They would have found something sooner or later. Even if Baz had managed to bring back every tank that still had a living specimen inside, it might not be enough.

Rachel Four was grown. She could give ten times the blood and a thousand times the DNA needed to stabilize his little girl.

She was the only option.

She trusted him. Loved him.

She would want to help him if he explained himself.

He could use that.

He pulled up her file.

It was dangerous to hack into FUC systems. Thankfully,

even after Mother's plans had all gone to shit, John's brief loyalties to her, and his former status as a student at FUCN'A, had provided Baz with a wonderful treasure trove of information.

He didn't need to hack their systems to know which properties FUC owned and used for either sting operations or housing students.

It wasn't difficult to figure out that Rachel would be in one of those properties. Being watched, yes, and that snake shifter with her would pose a problem...

There were no two ways about it.

Bazyli would be found, definitely arrested, if he was not killed first.

But he needed her for this.

She would understand. His other little girl would help him.

He just had to figure out how to get to her first.

13

Matthew didn't know much about what he was doing.

TJ didn't seem to have any complaints, however. Which was good. Matthew used that to guide him.

That, and doing everything that felt right and good. Everything he wanted to do TJ seemed to like.

And Matthew had thought many nights about what it would feel like to have TJ's dick in his mouth. He'd thought about the taste of it, the length of it, how TJ would sound when he kissed the length of his cock and sucked on the head.

TJ was flat on his bed. Matthew lay between his legs. He was eager to begin.

The moment Matthew started, he lost all sense of unease, all worry that he wasn't doing it right.

Aside from keeping his breathing even, and keeping his teeth as far away from the sensitive flesh as possible, it seemed quite simple.

And he *loved* the feeling of TJ's fingers gripping his hair. Loved the way he tried thrusting deeper into Matthew's mouth.

And Matthew especially loved the sound of each little gasp, and the way his name sounded on TJ's lips.

"Jesus, Matt, *fuuuuuck*." TJ arched his spine then fell flat to his back. He reached for one of the pillows, and Matthew took it as the height of all compliments when TJ tried to smother himself with it.

Matthew chuckled, needing to pull back. At some point he'd shoved TJ's shirt up, exposing his flat belly, the soft hairs that guided him down to TJ's cock and balls. His shorts were down just enough that they still hung around his knees while Matthew made him squirm.

He looked fucking divine like that. Body flushed, chest heaving, eyes confused and blown out with lust as he blinked down at Matthew, confused.

"What? What's... Are you okay?"

Matthew shook himself, wiping his mouth with the back of his hand. "Nothing. You are just—" *Adorable, too cute for words, taking my breath away.* "Nothing."

"Oh." TJ swallowed, nodding.

Was he embarrassed to be exposed like this?

Matthew, looking him right in the eye, wrapped his hand around the base of TJ's cock.

TJ sucked in a breath, his eyes drooping to half-mast while his shaft jumped in Matthew's hand.

"Does that feel good?"

He already knew the answer.

TJ pressed his lips together. He nodded.

That displeased Matthew. "Use your words," he said.

No, commanded.

He leaned in, giving TJ a show as he let the flat of his tongue slide across the head, pushing gently against the tip and slit.

TJ hissed.

Matthew pulled back.

Was TJ in pain? Matthew was trying to avoid the cast, but TJ kept clenching his knees and legs.

"Don't stop," TJ said, rubbing his palms over his face. "Fuck, please don't stop doing that."

Matthew was glad he was on his belly, his cock trapped between his body and the mattress. Otherwise, he might've come from the sound of that desperate voice alone.

God, what was wrong with him?

He wanted to control and dominate TJ. At the same time, that voice commanded something within him to become the man's servant. To give him everything he demanded.

So Matthew did. He kissed down the length of TJ's prick to the base, inhaling the musky, thick scent of him. Matthew couldn't say what prompted him to put TJ's testicle in his mouth, but he did it, and TJ really seemed to like that.

He arched almost entirely off the bed. Matthew was forced to push him back down by the belly.

TJ couldn't do that. He would hurt himself if he continued putting too much pressure on his leg.

TJ kept right on squirming, not taking the hint, even when Matthew growled around his mouthful. It was interfering with the important work Matthew needed to do, so he finally pulled back again.

"If you don't stop that, I'm going to tie you down."

Perhaps that was a bit harsh. TJ's eyes flew wide. He stared down at Matthew like he was a stranger.

Matthew should take it back. He shouldn't say such things.

But then TJ asked, "You want to? I mean... you can... if you... I don't think I've got anything you could use though."

"What?"

"You can use one of my ties," TJ said. "I've got a few in my closet. Never had the chance to use them before."

TJ wanted him to tie him down?

Instead of TJ being disgusted by the idea of doing such a thing, his eyes glimmered with interest.

And Matthew found himself wanting to see TJ like that. To see him belonging to no one else but him, to have his trust.

He jumped up. "In the closet, you said?"

TJ pushed himself to his elbows, cheeks flushed, lips parted and hair wonderfully messy. "Yeah. Uh, I've got some condoms in my bathroom, too."

Matthew froze just as he opened the closet door.

He got control quickly, hopefully quick enough that TJ didn't notice his sudden pause. "Of course."

He was inexperienced but not that uninformed.

Regardless, he had no reason to feel jealous. TJ was here with him now.

The Internet at the compound had been restricted. It had been more of an Intranet, but a former employee, someone who perhaps worked for his father before the place had been largely abandoned to Baz's whims, had brought a few magazines to his workspace.

Matthew had found them, been fascinated by them, and decided to keep them. For his own research. Luckily, even though the previous owner had made a somewhat question-able decision in bringing material such as that to a work setting, it had been a decision that clinically helped Matthew.

Matthew had been able to find proper sexual education materials within the local intranet. Condoms had been part of that study. He supposed the sexual function and reproduction materials would have to be on hand, considering the medical nature of the lab.

He shook the unpleasant thoughts from his head. He didn't want to think about that. He was here, with TJ, his inner owl preening and dancing at the thought of being with him.

Of taking him.

Heat rushed throughout his body. Matthew's hands trembled as he opened the bathroom drawer and grabbed the box of condoms and even a small bottle of lubricant.

He wasn't nervous, though.

More eager.

Matthew was also oddly pleased to see the box, and the little bottle, were both sealed.

TJ hadn't had anyone here. At least not recently.

Good. If Matthew had it his way, TJ wouldn't again for a long time.

Ever, hissed a little voice in his head. *Mine*.

He looked at himself in the mirror.

Quickly, he decided to undress, letting his clothing drop to the floor. He left them there, returning to TJ's bedroom entirely naked.

TJ seemed to be struggling to get his shorts off the thick cast around his lower leg. He paused at the sight of Matthew.

Matthew could hear the uneven thumping of the man's heart as he approached the bed. TJ's lips quirked up in a nervous kind of way.

"Are you scared?"

TJ shook his head. "No. Was just thinking it makes sense."

Matthew didn't understand. He climbed into bed, still careful to avoid TJ's cast, box and bottle in his hands.

"What I mean is," TJ explained, "you're an owl. I'm a fish. I feel kind of like you're about to eat me up."

"Again?"

TJ sputtered a laugh. He shook his head, pinching the bridge between his eyes. "Sure, yeah. If that's how you want to think about it."

Matthew did. He also wanted to kiss TJ again, so he did that, too.

TJ's hands settled onto his shoulders. Matthew liked that. He wanted TJ touching him everywhere.

But something wasn't right.

Matthew pulled back, glanced around, and frowned.

"Do you have more pillows?"

TJ looked confused, which was an interesting expression on the face of a man with his hard dick exposed. "Uh, not really, no?"

"Any more blankets?"

"Yeah, in the hallway closet. Why do you—?"

Matthew was already gone.

It was another one of those instincts he couldn't explain, something strong and surging inside him, demanding that he take control and make a proper space for TJ.

For them.

He grabbed the blankets. They weren't thick and fluffy like he'd hoped, but they would do. Soon they would smell of the two of them, and that made Matthew happy.

He brought them back to bed. TJ still had that confused look on his face. Some of the sheets pooled in his lap, as if to give himself some privacy.

"What are you up to?" TJ asked.

"Put your leg up." Matthew bundled one of the blankets, gently easing it beneath TJ's ankle so it was at least raised at some sort of angle.

The rest he rolled up as well, putting them on either side of TJ, blocking him into a cozy little space in the bed.

TJ relaxed the more he watched Matthew work.

"Making a nest for us?"

Was that what he was doing?

Matthew stopped when he was finished, surveying his works, a sense of pride and pleasure making his chest puff out. "Yes."

A nest. That was exactly what this was. And he wanted TJ to be comfortable inside it.

"Do you like it?"

"Not that I entirely understand the need," TJ said, glancing around then back up at Matthew, cheeks pink again, "But, yeah, I like it."

Matthew preened. He kissed TJ again.

"No more interruptions this time?" TJ asked between kisses.

Matthew shook his head. TJ's thighs parted for him easily. "No."

There was nothing else. They had everything they needed, and Matthew ached to be inside him.

"Just do me a favor," TJ said. "One last thing. Uh, don't go slamming too hard. It's been a while."

"Of course." Matthew had every intention of taking their pleasure slowly anyway. He knew this part could be painful if no care was taken. He wanted TJ to feel good.

But then, an idea occurred to him. "You can... to me, if you like."

TJ jerked back, a shocked sound escaping him. "Really?"

This was another one of those things Matthew did not understand. "Should we not?"

"No, I just... didn't expect you to offer."

"Why not?"

"I…" TJ seemed to think on that, apparently coming up short. "Nothing. I was just being dumb."

"No, you were not." Matthew leaned in. It had been too many long minutes without more touching, more kissing. He kissed TJ's collarbone. It seemed to be calling out to him the most.

"I mean it," he said, his voice low. "You can take me. I don't want to hurt you."

"You couldn't," TJ said, voice choked. "No, you do it. This is your first time, right?"

Matthew hated the reminder, but he nodded.

He wished he was more experienced. He almost felt like he should be, though he wasn't sure why.

"Then you should top." He grinned impishly. "We can work up to you being the bottom later."

Work up to it. Meaning there would be another time.

That sounded fucking perfect, and there was only so much patience in Matthew's body, so much he could stop or hesitate, even for TJ's benefit. If this was what TJ wanted, then it was what he wanted.

He reached for the lubricant.

"Tell me if I hurt you." That was his only command.

"Sure," TJ said, leaning back. "You forgot to tie me up."

Oh. So he had.

They looked at each other. They laughed together. Matthew popped the cap of the bottle.

"We'll try that later." Now seemed like a time to keep things simple.

It was slippery in his hands. He expected that. He stroked it between his fingers and brought his blunt nails to TJ's rim.

He wished he could stare into TJ's eyes for that, but this seemed like a task he needed to focus on.

He glanced back and forth, between his fingers and TJ's face. Watching for signs of discomfort. TJ told him to wait when he needed a moment then sighed and allowed Matthew another finger to stretch him open with.

He was so tight. Matthew's cock ached to feel that same clench his fingers got.

"I'm going to humiliate myself when I'm in you," he gritted out, hoping to give TJ some warning in case he disappointed him. "Fuck, I'll come right away."

TJ gasped softly, his hands clenching into the nest Matthew built for them. "I wouldn't mind."

He sounded like he meant it.

Matthew loved him for that.

He loved him entirely.

Matthew kissed him again, thrusting his fingers slowly forward and back, bit by bit. Whatever TJ's body would allow him to have, he took.

Then he hooked his fingers and seemed to find a perfect spot, because TJ arched his spine and shouted.

There. Matthew made a mental note of that spot.

"Fuck," TJ groaned. "Stop, stop, stop."

What?

Matthew quickly pulled back, searching for a sign he'd hurt the man.

"Are you—?"

"I'm fine. I got it." TJ was already half twisted onto his side. He reached for the condom.

With a practiced ease Matthew was a little jealous of, he tore the packet open.

"We need to speed this up."

Matthew sucked in a quick breath as TJ slid the condom down the length of his cock.

TJ was still smiling, still handsome and eager. "Because

now I'm worried I'll come a little too quick if you keep doing that with your fingers."

"Really?" Matthew's ego swelled as his cock throbbed.

TJ leaned back, his arm slipping above his head, his other hand resting on his belly. "I mean, yeah."

Matthew never thought he would feel as happy as this. This was beyond anything he thought he deserved.

He just hoped he would satisfy. That this wouldn't disappoint.

He pressed the head against TJ's rim, and fuck if that already didn't feel so good.

He had to pause, to take a breath.

"Take your time." TJ's hands found their way to Matthew's hips. "You got this."

Matthew gritted his teeth. Not yet he didn't, but when he was sure he wouldn't come the instant he was sheathed, he slowly, slowly, slowly inched his way forward.

TJ was tight. He felt hot and soft everywhere. The grip of him around Matthew's shaft created the sort of shiver-inducing deliciousness he'd never thought possible.

"God... damn," he growled.

He was suddenly at the furthest depth. He could go no farther. TJ had taken him to the hilt, his arms around Matthew's shoulders, body tense.

"Are you okay?"

"Yeah." TJ exhaled hard. "One second. Give me one... been a while."

Matthew nodded. He'd give TJ his fucking soul right now. Anything and everything he had TJ could demand from him and Matthew would hand it over without a second thought. So long as he could stay like this.

He wanted to move. Everything inside Matthew screamed

to start canting his hips forward and back. He clenched his toes and pressed his eyes and nose into the crook of TJ's neck until he felt the man's body relax beneath him.

A soft exhale. A gentle press of long fingers through Matthew's hair.

Then a warm whisper in his ear. "Move, baby. Give it to me."

Holy shit.

A switch was suddenly flipped.

Matthew growled low in his throat, the animal side of his brain taking almost full control. He barely remembered to be careful of TJ's leg as he gripped TJ's hips, fucking into him hard and quick.

TJ threw his head back and shouted a sound that went to Matthew's groin and spurned him on quicker.

Harder. Deeper.

Even with this wild, untamed side of his brain taking over, he knew he could be better. He knew his movements were clumsy.

TJ didn't seem to mind. He thrust his hips back to meet Matthew, their flesh smacking together in a lewd noise Matthew loved.

He loved their smell. Loved TJ's soft, sweaty skin over firm muscle. Loved how tight he was around Matthew's cock.

His end was already in sight.

Matthew growled, pressing biting kisses along TJ's neck and shoulder.

Every shred of willpower, every inch of self-control he had, couldn't stop that building inside him. That flight over the cliff and the dive that would follow.

Stronger than even his instinct to hunt when he caught

sight of a rabbit hundreds of feet below him. Stronger than the need to breathe, he was coming.

"Come inside me." TJ gripped his hair, painfully tight, growling again into his ear. "Mark me."

Matthew groaned.

He came. He came, and he felt ashamed and whole and wonderful at the same time.

He rocked through his orgasm, hating the condom between them, wanting to put his scent, and his seed, all over TJ's body. Inside him.

As if he would warn away other predators.

TJ moaned and squirmed beneath him, rocking his hips, thrusting against Matthew's still-hard cock.

"Oh fuck. Please, please, please," he begged.

Fuck. A new shame hit him. Was Matthew supposed to make TJ come first? He wasn't sure if he had that ability, but it seemed suddenly important that he fix it.

He wrapped his hand around TJ's still throbbing shaft, stroking from root to tip.

It still felt good, having TJ rocking against him. Seeing him like this while Matthew came down off that wonderful high.

"That's it," Matthew said. "I'll take care of you. I got you."

He reached for the little bottle, quickly adding more of the slick to his hands before wrapping both of them around TJ's prick. Both fists together were just enough to cover the entire thing, to give TJ something warm and tight to thrust into.

He did, with such wild abandon it made Matthew's cock twitch with interest while still inside him.

"Come for me." It seemed like the right thing to say. "You're so hot like this. Come on…"

TJ covered his mouth with his hands, shouting into them.

Matthew didn't like that. He wished he could hear it, but then he grunted and shivered as TJ's hole clenched around him, so tight and forceful. A splash of wet heat coated Matthew's hands.

TJ exhaled hard, flopping onto the bed.

The air between them was suddenly different. Their heavy breathing, thick musk between them. Matthew felt calmer. Able to think more clearly.

His dick was certainly no longer calling the shots and commanding his attention.

He was a little shocked.

He'd just had sex with TJ. Just admitted, at least to himself, that he loved him. Now he was on top of the guy, still inside him, hiding his face in TJ's shoulder thinking about how good he still smelled. How nice it felt to press his lips to TJ's collarbone.

"Are you okay?"

Matthew snorted and pulled back. "I should ask you that."

TJ's mouth quirked. Matthew twisted his body slightly before realizing they were still joined and he was trapped.

"I'm great," he replied. "This was more than great."

"Was it?" Matthew smiled, his cock flexing in response.

"Gah! Stop that!" TJ laughed. "I can only take so much. Ow, let me up. My good leg is cramping."

He assisted TJ to the bathroom so he could clean himself up. Matthew wished he wouldn't. He liked his scent on the other man, but it did feel good to wash his hands and toss the used condom into the little trash bin before he gave TJ some privacy.

He didn't want to get dressed, but he also wasn't sure of

the etiquette here, so Matthew satisfied himself with pants only. He refreshed the nest, then remembered the food, once again becoming overcome with the need to feed the man.

As well as other things.

When he heard the tap running, Matthew quickly checked the Internet on his phone and typed in, *owl mating habits.*

He took a deep breath, held it, and let it out slowly. It turned out, creating comfortable sleeping spaces and providing food were quite normal actions for an owl when wooing a mate.

He looked around. The paper bags filled with food he'd set on TJ's nightstand. This strange feeling in his chest at the thought of TJ being so much as uncomfortable with anything.

Yes. Clearly, this was what he was doing. It was the only thing that made sense.

However, just because he was trying to make a mate out of the man did not mean TJ wanted anything to do with that.

Matthew didn't know much about casual sex, or dating in general, but he wasn't stupid.

The fact that he loved TJ did not mean TJ would love him back. That they'd had sex, while excellent and Matthew wanted more, did not make a mating.

TJ opened the bathroom door. He was in a loose pair of boxers, something he'd been able to get over the cast, and leaning against the wall while he eased himself forward.

"Sorry. Did I keep you waiting?"

Matthew tossed his phone to the side. He rushed to TJ's side, assisting him back to bed.

TJ huffed. "I don't need this much help," he said, accepting Matthew's arm anyway.

Matthew liked that. He liked feeling useful, that he could protect and assist TJ. "I know. I should feed you, though."

"Good. I'm starving."

That pleased Matthew as well.

He loved watching TJ eat the food he'd paid for with FUC's money. He loved that the sheets still smelled pleasantly of their coupling.

He also loved when TJ pulled him onto the mattress to lie down together after the food was finished, the both of them drinking from their paper cups in each other's arms.

"Just so you know," TJ said, "I don't normally eat in bed. I'm just being lazy today."

There was a television in front of them. It was off. Neither made a move to turn it on.

"That's fine." Matthew didn't care what bad habits TJ got up to in his own time.

He didn't even care if the man didn't love him back.

TJ definitely liked him. That much was a given. Matthew could live with that. He could be happy with that.

For now.

If TJ decided he no longer wanted to have sex or be friends, Matthew would accept it. Would let him go.

Even if it broke his damn heart.

14

The sex continued for several more days.

FUC contacted Matt multiple times between rounds in the bedroom, which TJ hated.

It annoyed him they were calling Matt away so much to answer questions, to look over the compound again, especially since TJ couldn't be there with him when he had the stupid cast on his leg.

That irritated him the most.

It was like they were using Matt to try and make a map of that underground lair he'd been in. Not that TJ knew what use that would be when half the thing had fallen down on them already.

He didn't think they were making Rachel do that same work, but TJ was afraid to ask. He didn't want to come across as bitter about it or dump extra work into her lap.

He knew Matt didn't want her back at that compound anyway. He didn't blame the guy for that, but he also knew Matt had yet to tell her about the tanks or that she was likely one of many clone daughters Bazyli had created in those underground labs.

That was also something TJ didn't bring up.

He didn't want to fight, and every time Matt returned to TJ's house, more food bags in his arms, and occasionally even gifting extra comfy blankets and pillows, TJ was too happy to see him.

Too eager to break the mood and invite Matthew back to his bed.

And hot damn, was the man ever a quick study. The sex was fucking awesome.

TJ was a little embarrassed with himself by how much he liked it. He didn't think he could like bottoming this much.

It had, at first, started out as doing Matt a favor, letting him take control since it was his first time, but it quickly turned into selfish little pleasure sessions for TJ because, well, when the student was doing so well in his studies, it was best not to interrupt him.

Not that Matthew didn't offer. He did, often, but now TJ was the one worried that he'd disappoint.

Just because he wasn't a virgin didn't mean he had much experience, after all.

They were lying in the nest Matthew had built for them one night. The TV turned on, but TJ couldn't say what was playing, still buzzed from another round of awesome sex and adoring the feeling of Matt's fingers toying around in his hair, when TJ asked, "Why do you keep making these nests?"

Matt tensed, the vibe instantly changing.

"Sorry," TJ said quickly. "If it's an instinct thing, I won't ask."

"It is," Matt said quickly, his cheeks coloring as he scratched the back of his neck, the picture of discomfort. "An instinct thing. I looked into it."

"You don't have to be embarrassed," TJ said. "I know people have different instincts, depending on the animal you turn into."

"Right," Matt growled, though he pulled TJ closer, which TJ liked.

"I'm serious. Blankets and pillows aren't the worst thing I've ever heard of."

"Really?" Matt seemed interested then. "What else have you heard of?"

"Well..." TJ thought quickly. He didn't have to struggle to come up with something. "When I was living at FUCN'A, we heard of this panda shifter who ate a whole set of bamboo furniture."

"What? No, you didn't," Matt scoffed, but he was smiling.

TJ practically flopped onto his chest. His cast was close to coming off. He thought he could take it off today, but his appointment wasn't until tomorrow. Either way, he was feeling better and better, skin to skin with Matt. "I'm serious! And Bobby used to spit webbing all over his bed. It, uh, freaked out his roommate."

"I saw him do that." Matt shivered. "Like he was trying to catch something to eat."

"Or make a more comfortable place to sleep," TJ said. He was still mad at Bobby but didn't want to talk badly about a dead man, either. "So, you see? Making a nice, cozy place to have sex and snooze in is pretty awesome."

Matthew seemed satisfied, relieved. Did he really think TJ would be bothered?

Maybe he should look into owl instincts. If Matt was spending pretty much every night at TJ's house already, and if he was getting ready to sleep for the winter or something, then maybe TJ should have a talk with him about staying here full-time.

He didn't want the guy alone at his apartment, sleeping for twenty-three hours a day, skipping meals and everything else. Did owls sleep during the winter? Or did they fly somewhere else? TJ was pretty sure he'd never seen an owl in the winter, but he could be wrong about that.

Wait, no, that was dumb. Even if owls hibernated, Matt wasn't a real owl. He was a shifter. His animal instincts only had so much of a hold on him.

Whenever he was cuddled up in Matt's enormous arms, he felt exactly zero need to study shifter behaviors anyway. To do anything other than lazily listen to the man's heartbeat and let Matt feed him. The guy insisted on doing all the providing.

Yeah, TJ liked having Matt in his house.

The next day, after one last X-ray, his cast finally, finally, came off.

Matt was back at the compound, helping FUC agents to map out the facility again, but TJ was more than able to drive himself.

He all but ran into her clinic. His leg had felt fine for a while, except it was stupidly itchy, and he was eager to wear real pants again.

He brought a pair to the clinic just for the occasion.

"You're in a good mood," she said, grinning as TJ hopped neatly onto the examination table, X-ray completed and the results happily in.

"Very good." He stuck his leg out. "Please get this off me. I'm dying."

"Yes, I'm sorry, it must have been difficult." She moved toward a metal tray, some tools already arranged on top.

He was on cloud nine. "No, I'm good. A few days was hard enough. I'd've pulled out my hair and gone bald if I had to wear this for several weeks."

She laughed, pulling out a scary-looking saw from the tray. "Of course. My mistake. Hold still."

She froze suddenly, her nostrils flaring just slightly. "Have you...?" She didn't finish, the question remained unasked and hanging in the air.

TJ frowned, tensed. He sniffed under his arm real quick. "What?"

Diane tilted her head just a little, the saw still in her gloved hands. "Has Matthew been spending more time with you?"

TJ tensed. "Is that a problem? I didn't think it would be a conflict of interest if he was at my house anymore since he's working for FUC now and no longer a wanted man."

In truth, he wasn't sure he wanted anyone knowing they were banging each other like a couple of rabbit shifters either. It was just... personal. He also didn't know how Matt would feel either, if everyone knew what they were up to.

"Not a problem and not a conflict of interest," Diane said. "I'm sorry. I shouldn't have asked."

She turned the little buzz saw on, which screeched to life with a scary-sounding scream that made TJ jump a little. Then he held very, *very* still.

Only when she started cutting into the material did the scent whoosh up into his own nose.

Dry cloth particles and plaster dust.

And something else.

Oh God.

He wanted to throw himself into a hole and die. That smell... Of course Diane knew. Jesus.

He'd thought he was being careful. He still bathed, obviously, and wore fresh, clean clothes everywhere, but of course, their scents would have stayed on the stupid cast. He should have known. Maybe he'd gone scent-blind to it after so many days, longer than any shifter, even a lab experiment like him, needed for healing.

His whole face and body felt hot. He totally forgot to be worried about the little buzz saw or the scissors when those came out next.

His leg felt cold and clammy when it was finally free. He rolled his ankle and reached down to rub his hands along his hairy leg. Anything to not have to look at Diane.

"For what it's worth," Diane said, tossing the remains of his cast into a bin, "I'm very glad you're both together."

"Yeah?" He didn't get it. "Why?"

She pulled her gloves off with a little snap next, heaving a sigh. "It's hard enough to be a shifter in the world these days. Too much shit to deal with, too many humans who know. Who want to be like us."

Shame caught TJ in his guts once again. He'd been one of those humans once upon a time.

"That's not a comment on you," she said softly, knowing full well where his thoughts had gone. "Or anyone else who gets... sucked into all of this, but there is a lot to keep up with. It's not remotely any of my business, but I think you're both good for each other."

"Oh..." That was... kind of nice to hear. "Because we can watch out for each other? Because we're both... experiments?"

He still wasn't entirely sure if that's what Matt was, but it was the likely explanation and the one the people of FUC seemed to be working with.

"Yes. You can also make some more friends. They can do that for you, too, but having a mate is... special. Not everyone gets that. You deserve someone like that." She paused. "The both of you do."

Mate? What the actual fuck?

TJ cleared his suddenly dry throat. There was no air in the room. He didn't have conversations quite like this.

Ever.

No one had ever told him he was worthy of things like this.

Except maybe Matt, which was nice but also new to him and kind of uncomfortable at times.

He liked Diane, but he didn't know her nearly as well as he knew Matt.

Then there was the whole mate thing.

He wasn't a real shifter. Just a made-up one in a lab.

"Are you all right? TJ?"

"Oh..." He tensed slightly, caught in his thoughts again. "Uh, I don't think we're mates."

"No?" Diane lifted a brow at him. She looked almost amused.

He tensed. The heat under his collar was unbearable. Was she serious? Just because he and Matt were... just because Matt was spending a lot of time at his house...

Was that how it worked in the shifter world?

"All right, not mates, just extra special friends," Diane said, taking pity on him. There was a little smile on her face as she scratched something off on her clipboard.

Holy shit. Was he mating with Matt? That sort of implied something permanent. That was how every other shifter he talked to spoke about mating.

He was in a doctor's office, after all. He should ask right now.

"You're good to go. I'll leave, and you can put those pants on I know you brought. If anything changes, call me. I want to know all the details of how you recover and what your healing abilities are like."

He nodded, throat dry as fuck. He couldn't even bring himself to be annoyed over the fact that he was still something of a curious experiment even to the people of FUC. At least this was all for his health, not someone else's crazy scam.

His mind whirled as he jumped off the table. "Wait, uh, before you go, I have a question."

Diane looked back at him and then gently shut the door again. "Of course."

TJ suddenly didn't know what to do with his hands. "How would I know if I was mating with someone? Or already mated? How does that work?"

Diane's brows lifted. TJ felt like he'd just asked her about the birds and the bees.

"Well, it's a little different for each shifter. Sometimes animal type comes into play, of course."

"Right, but is it like a choice you make when you want a partner or something that just"—he snapped his fingers— "clicks and you know?"

He'd heard all kinds of things.

That same, gentle smile tugged at her lips. "Some people just know. They catch sight of their mate across the room. A man might smell his woman at a distance if there's blood at play."

"Oh, you mean like during a hunt? If she cuts herself?"

Her smile turned a little mischievous. "Or during her cycle."

Christ.

"Right, so, uh, blood. At this point I've probably bled in front of Matt a few times, but I don't think it was anything like that."

He'd definitely sustained more than a few cuts and scrapes when he was kidnapped and brought to that facility where Matt lived then the fall in that secret room in the same underground bunker.

Not to mention Matt's healing burns from that time. TJ had smelled his blood to be sure, and he hadn't flown into an uncontrollable need to suck the man's dick.

But now that he was thinking about that...

He cleared his throat.

"It doesn't have to be blood. Or at first sight," Diane said. "That is definitely true. Sometimes it hits a little slower, but if it's right, if your instincts call out and answer each other, it can take."

TJ thought of his animal, a horrific-looking fish thing. He didn't think it had the instinct to do anything other than find small, helpless prey at the bottom of the ocean to sneak up on and eat. Or distract with that bulb of light it created.

Matt, however, was a beautiful, majestic, *huge* owl.

He could fly and had beautiful feathers that TJ longed to stroke and touch.

He was just too embarrassed to ask.

Yeah... if Matt was in the middle of mating him, or already was, he'd definitely gotten the shorter end of that stick.

A gentle hand pressed on his shoulder, shocking him out of his thoughts once again.

Diane held her clipboard against her chest with her other hand. The look on her face was almost sympathetic.

A reminder that he'd been in a room similar to this one too many times after FUC found him. She and Nolan had seen him at his worst. Had seen his huge, ugly, needle-like teeth as they stretched his lips to the point where they cracked and bled. He'd stabbed himself in the gums regularly. He'd constantly needed smelly creams and terrible-tasting toothpaste for the cuts in and around his mouth. Most people refused to look him in his bulbous eyes.

She hadn't done that. The worst she'd done was pause slightly when she saw him the first time. Each interaction, each instance of medical care he'd needed, she had always been warm and kind. To the point where he'd broken down and cried in her arms.

More than once.

He felt that vibe from her now.

Unlike those other times, he manned up and resisted the urge to cry, though his throat still got tight.

"There's nothing wrong with you," she said.

"Yeah, well—"

"No, none of that." Her hand gripped his shoulder tighter. "There is nothing wrong with you. If you and Matt have something happening, then don't let the idea of a mating scare you off. Just see where this goes. It could be a fun fling, or it could be something deeper. You deserve to enjoy it, regardless."

"What do you think it is?"

"Honestly?" She pulled her hand back from his shoulder, surveying him like she was proud. "I think whatever it between you is for the two of you to discover together."

TJ exhaled long and deep.

"Of course."

15

Matthew was getting a little tired of returning to the pit, again and again and again.

The home that had once felt so safe, his hiding place from the world, where he and his sister slept, looked more like a hole in the ground. Seeing it now, with so much time between then and now, Matthew's burn scars fading but still tingling, just made it look ugly and depressing.

There was no trace of the little nook where he'd made his bed and used to sleep. Anything that had formerly belonged to Rachel was either crushed or burned to a crisp. Which was a shame. She hadn't owned much. Neither of them had, but he would have liked to bring her some things.

Maybe it was for the best.

A full fresh start. Nothing to remind her of this horrible place. Aside from Matthew, that was.

He didn't like to admit it, but her relationship with the snake shifter was probably the best thing to have happened to her. Matthew could now admit that it was his arrival in the compound that was the catalyst to all of this. To setting him and his sister free.

She deserved that. Deserved someone smart, who could keep her safe.

That, and the fact that John was a cobra, able to sneak around and surprise any danger to her, able to bite and poison her enemies, made Matt feel a touch jealous.

He hadn't realized it before, but it was jealousy.

Someone better could care for Rachel. Could protect her and give her a normal life.

Meanwhile, Matthew's owl shape was so oversized that he couldn't go flying during the day, lest someone see him. So big that he could barely fly out of the little hole he and TJ had fallen into.

He still didn't like that he'd been unable to take TJ into his talons and fly him out.

Thank God TJ was the sort of shifter who could create that bulb of light, so Matthew didn't have to feel extra terrible about leaving him in the dark.

Still, even as he kicked around the debris, searching for signs of any equipment that was still salvageable, something FUC could study so they could prevent something like this from happening again, he couldn't help but smile.

His relationship with TJ was progressing, to say the least.

There was... a lot of sex.

And when there wasn't sex, there was cuddling in the blankets and pillows Matthew arranged for him in bed in front of the TV. They were currently on a *John Wick* movie binge and would soon be watching *The Continental.*

He loved those moments.

He loved sex almost as much. Loved that he could make TJ feel good. Loved the smell of the man as he threw his head back and exposed his throat when he came as Matthew was inside him.

It was definitely a relief that his first time wasn't terrible for the man. And even more wonderful that TJ continued to let him improve his skills.

Not that he'd had any complaints.

Still, even without the sex, there was something comforting and warm about having TJ in bed with him, in his arms, his head on Matt's chest. He never said it out loud, but Matthew was convinced TJ was listening to his heart. The position of his ear was always a little too perfect.

Matthew couldn't wait to get out of here today, out of his damp, smelly concrete wreck, shower the scent of this dead place off of him, and get back into that nest with TJ.

With his mate.

If only he could admit to TJ that he wished to make him a mate. He didn't know if there was anything he was supposed to do about it. Should he tell TJ? Was it too soon?

The more Matthew looked into mating habits, the more people he asked, the more clear it became that this was something Matthew was experiencing. He wanted TJ as his mate—as his permanent life partner—but he had no clue how to tell the man this or if it would be appropriate to bring it up to him.

TJ could simply like him as a good friend. Hell, even as a lover, someone he cared for. That didn't mean TJ would wish to spend his life with him.

Matthew sighed. He pushed over a blackened box that likely had once been an old computer. It fell off its wobbly perch and burst into black dust, plastic, and glass.

He wished he could get out of here.

"Not finding anything?"

He whirled around. Matthew hadn't heard anyone sneaking up on him.

That unnerved him. He should have been more alert.

The tall man in glasses and a protective face mask didn't seem threatening. He looked around as though he would also prefer to be somewhere else. His jumpsuit and gloves were not covered in soot, not wet from anything either. He looked like he'd just put them on to come down for his shift.

The guy looked around and then locked eyes with Matthew. "It's kind of depressing."

No shit. "Have we met?"

The man looked familiar. There were a number of FUC agents Matthew had come across since he'd been forced into the group. He couldn't have had proper introductions with everyone, and there were usually quite a few people on-site here.

That, and the mask didn't help either.

He was startled when the man began lowering his.

Matthew frowned. "What are you doing?" He did not lower his mask in kind. They weren't supposed to. The air was not clean.

Regardless, the man showed Matthew his whole face. "My name's Albert. I work with FUC."

"Obviously, but you should put your mask back on."

Albert frowned slightly. He didn't appear angry. He seemed more... thoughtful. "What's your name?"

"Matthew." Only Rachel and TJ called him Matt, and he didn't know this guy, so he didn't offer that name.

"You're an owl shifter?"

Now Matthew frowned. "Yeah."

"I am, too." He took a step forward. "I was told to come and speak with you. That I might be... helpful to you."

Matthew was already interested. He stepped forward. "You're an owl shifter? Really?"

That was exciting news. He'd met so many shifters around FUC. Cat shifters, both wild and domestic like Sam and Steve. He even met a woman who had what looked like a unicorn horn popping out of her forehead. A wolf shifter and even a panda shifter who claimed to have once been a kangaroo.

There were even a few bird shifters, but he'd not met an owl.

That was exciting. Someone like him. Someone who could tell him what was going on with himself, if the man was open to a conversation.

Albert smiled, and then he lifted the mask back over his mouth. Matthew thought it might be that he couldn't handle breathing in this damp odor anymore. "Yes, I was given permission to introduce myself to you. Do you want to come up and chat for a bit?"

"God, yes."

Matthew was dying to get out of there. He hated the smell, and though he was technically working for FUC— being paid, and even had a lanyard with his name and status as an employee of FUC on it—he couldn't help but think he was still down here every day as a form of punishment or, at the very least, a gentle hazing for his time as a stooge for the bad guys.

His acceptance seemed to please Albert very much. "All right. Let's go."

They moved out of the damp space, their boots making wet, squishing noises as they trekked through the wet muck.

It turned out that the compound had been built over a clay-heavy area. Matthew hadn't known that when he'd lived here. Now, he hated it. The fires and explosion had opened rooms deeper in the facility he hadn't known existed. The concrete flooring had either not been put down or it had broken open during the fires and explosions, leaving messy, wet clay everywhere that stuck to everything.

Thankfully, ever since TJ's fall, FUC had been quick to work on the structure of the compound. They reinforced areas, ensuring the place was sound, and the elevators that could be repaired were now running on the generators up top.

Matthew and Albert rode one to the ground floor and he was happy to rip off his mask when they were up top, where the sun illuminated everything from the parked FUC vehicles to the many makeshift workspaces under canvas tarps.

No one stopped him as he and Albert walked away.

Sam glanced in his direction. The man was looking over more plans of the compound, but he simply nodded and went back to what he was doing.

Matthew felt a touch lighter.

Sometimes he hated having to go back down there, again and again, searching for materials he didn't even know existed. But times like this, he was glad he worked for these people.

Had they sent Albert down below for him, to speak to him about what it was like to be an owl shifter? He couldn't wait to learn more about what it meant. He didn't know this man, but Matthew wanted to ask him so many questions.

They stopped at one of the stations to drop off their protective gear. Albert was stripping out of his gloves, suit, and protective booties, revealing a normal set of clothes beneath. Jeans and sensible shoes, along with a sweater vest and pressed blue, button-down shirt.

The guy looked more like he belonged in an office setting.

Or a library.

"I'm hungry, and I wouldn't mind getting a coffee. Do you want anything?" Albert asked, looking back at him.

"I..." Matthew snapped out of it and pulled himself out

of his plastic, protective suit as well. Gloves and booties next.

His shoes were still filthy. Nothing could keep the clay off after a few hours down there. It seemed to get everywhere.

"No, maybe. I would really just like to speak with you."

"Did they tell you I was coming?" Albert asked. He nodded his thanks to the officer who took his and Matthew's suits for cleaning, and then they were on their way.

"No. No one did."

Matthew stopped next to what he believed was Albert's vehicle. The lights briefly flashed when Albert unlocked it.

Was he really going to get in this guy's car? It seemed... like something he shouldn't do. He'd just met the guy, and there were so many dangers in the world.

But no one had stopped them, and no one looked at Albert as though he was a threat.

"If you want to stay here, we can," Albert said, noticing Matthew's hesitation.

Matthew decided he wasn't going to be a pussy about this. "No. We can go." He opened the door and sat in the passenger side quickly.

Albert grinned, sitting in the driver's side and starting the engine.

They drove away from the compound and were soon on the highway.

"I'm Albert Huntly, by the way," Albert said. "I don't think I told you my last name."

Matthew wasn't sure why he needed it.

"I don't have a last name," he said. TJ hadn't told him his surname, but Matthew figured he wouldn't mind having it, whatever that was.

Albert nodded. "Yes, I figured. I'm very sorry about everything that's happened so far."

"It's fine." Matthew couldn't help but smile. "Things have been much better lately."

He reminded himself daily why it was worth it to go into that miserable pit every day, looking for things to salvage. He wasn't on the run anymore, sleeping in abandoned fishing shacks and struggling to hunt on his own with his huge owl shape that could barely be hidden, couldn't perch on trees without bending the whole thing over and scaring away all the prey.

Now, he had a job. He was in regular contact with Rachel, had food in his belly every night, and he barely stayed in that little apartment FUC had provided to him. He'd spent every night in TJ's bed.

And TJ was wonderful. He alone made the things he'd lived through—his time with his father, the fire, and the cold and hungry nights—worth it.

"Does it hurt?"

Matthew frowned. "Does what hurt?"

Albert, keeping his eyes on the road, gestured to his own face vaguely. Then he cringed, as though embarrassed to even point out the scarring.

"Oh, not anymore." Matthew resisted the urge to scratch it. "They don't bother me anymore, and this is much better considering what it used to be."

"Not much can hurt or scar us."

He nodded, thinking of TJ's cast. He wished he could have been there for his appointment with Diane to have it removed, but he was looking forward to getting home tonight and seeing him again.

"I'm likely not a real shifter," he said. "Like TJ, I was probably human before."

"And you're not sure who you were before the compound? Your life? Your family?"

"No." He thought this was common knowledge by now. He thought it would have been talked about, even if unofficially. Gossip traveled quickly.

"No. I woke up two years ago. Rachel was there, and so was... Bazyli."

Felt strange, not calling him *Father*, but he couldn't. Not anymore.

Albert nodded, his hands tightening on the wheel.

They drove into the town.

"Yeah... I want you to know there's a chance you could be related to me."

Matthew whipped his head to the side, staring at Albert. "Related to you? How?"

"Not sure."

The man lied.

Matthew didn't know how he knew, but he felt it. It seemed obvious. How could they be related and not know how?

Unless...

"Am I a distant cousin of yours or something?"

It was the only thing he could think of that made sense. Someone in the family that wasn't seen or spoken to often.

Matthew used to think family kept in contact, that everyone was close, the way he and Rachel would be. But he'd learned in his time outside that it wasn't always the case. People could have second and third cousins they barely knew of and hardly ever saw. Hell, they might have siblings and parents they never spoke to. It was how people like Bazyli, Mother, and, before both of them, Mastermind had taken so many people for their experiments.

"Or something. We're still looking into it," Albert said.

Another lie. They weren't just looking into it. It must be a certainty at this point for Albert to make contact and just walk off the job with him for a coffee run.

Albert knew something. They were connected somehow, but he wasn't ready to say it.

They pulled into the parking lot of the coffee shop, went inside, and Matthew was shocked when Albert insisted on paying for his drink and his pastry. He quickly whipped out his wallet and passed his card over the machine before Matthew had the chance to pay for himself.

"I got it. We have lots to talk about." Albert smiled at him.

It was tense, but he seemed sincere. Like he was trying to be friendly.

Matthew decided to give him a chance. "Thanks. I'll get you the next time."

He'd learned that was the polite thing to do. If a friend got the drinks once, then it would be his turn the next time.

Albert nodded. "All right. Let's go and sit. There's a quiet corner over there. I don't think anyone will hear us if we're quiet."

That was good. "Thanks for coming to see me. I'm... interested to learn more about owls."

And if they were related, then all the better.

Albert nodded, and they took seats. He pulled out his phone. "This is my wife. Beverly and the boy is my son, Finn."

Matthew looked at them. The woman was pretty, glowing. Finn seemed a happy child, sitting in his mother's arms with a green Hulk doll.

"He used to be more blond, but his hair's been getting darker, like his mother and I."

Albert looked at him and Matthew thought he was searching for something.

He smiled and handed back the phone. "Your family is beautiful."

"They are," Albert agreed, beaming. He was so proud.

Matthew hoped he could have that with TJ one day.

"Beverly is a beaver shifter, but she's large. With long saber teeth."

The *like you* went unsaid.

A new surge of excitement hit him.

But then, he frowned. Albert had said they might be related. He'd assumed that meant on Albert's side, hence the owls. But how could he be related to both of them? That made no sense.

Unless there was something weird happening in this family that he didn't want to know about. Or, maybe, Albert was just pointing it out if he wanted help with that side of things.

It was apparently out of the ordinary for shifters to be oversized like he was but not entirely rare. If he was related to Albert, and Albert was willing to introduce them, perhaps he could speak to Beverly at some point. She could give him an idea of how to be a shifter of his size without drawing attention to himself.

And, since this man had a mate, he would know more about the signs his animal side had given him. If Matthew was correct in believing TJ was his mate at all.

And what Matthew needed to do if TJ was.

He is.

"So, what would you like to know? I hear you're already a gifted flyer."

Matthew nodded, his arms on the table as he leaned forward and asked everything he'd ever wanted to ask.

16

TJ checked his messages when he got home.

Charlie and Trisha were planning a lunch and wanted to know if he wanted to be there. He wasn't so sure about that. He was thinking more about a specific kind of guy's time with Matt, but he replied back that he would check his plans.

No messages from Rachel or John, but he expected that. She was messaging him directly less and less now that she was able to speak freely with her brother. If she did want to tell him anything, it was now Matt she contacted and Matt who passed along the message.

That was fine. It was the way it should be.

Nothing from work, but he expected that, too. They would know the cast came off today—there was no hiding that from them—but he thought about making something up about his leg still being tender. That he needed just one more day at home. But TJ wanted to work. He wanted to prove he could be a useful employee to FUC.

With only some mild hesitation on his part, TJ sent a

notice to his supervisor at FUC that he could get started on more than paperwork.

However, he'd be lying to himself if he didn't admit that he liked lazing around in bed, in the nest Matt insisted on creating for him every night. He loved rolling around in their combined scents. He loved basking in the feeling of Matt's...

Love? Definitely affection.

Yes, that was an easier word. Love was too big for him to hope for.

TJ loved Matt. He wasn't sure when he came to that realization, but it was there. As simple and easy as waking up in the morning. It was an easy fact. Like looking out the window and seeing the sun shining. Just something that was.

TJ was in love with the big guy.

But thinking,—hoping—that Matt loved him back?

Too much pressure.

Matt definitely liked him. He smiled easily at TJ when they were in bed together. And when they weren't.

He threw his arm over TJ's shoulder when they were sitting together on the couch. They did most things at home, now that TJ thought about it.

There wasn't much to do in the small town where FUCN'A resided, aside from what was on the main strip, but the vast woods and hills surrounding the town itself were the real draws for the many shifters who lived here. The running, flying, and hunting were the main forms of entertainment.

Matt was too big to fly around even these thousands of acres of woods in the daylight, so that left nighttime for him.

But lately, their nights were spent at home, in bed together.

TJ wished, not for the first time, that he wasn't some giant, ugly, mutilated-looking fish thing. That he could run and hunt and enjoy the woods like the wolves and cats and bears who lived here. Then maybe he could run and hunt and play with Matt, even if it was only at night.

But maybe there was something he and Matt could do.

TJ quickly made the bed, putting down the fresh sheets he'd thrown in the dryer before his appointment with Diane. He loved it when Matt came back every night to bunch up the sheets and pillows to make that cozy nest for them.

He did a quick scroll on Amazon next and clicked the Buy Now button on a few expensive things he probably shouldn't splurge on right now, but they'd be a fun surprise for Matt.

A buzz came into his phone. Matt.

TJ's heart warmed. The man apologized for not contacting him sooner and asked how his appointment went. He replied back that it was all right and he was back at home. Then, after a brief pause, he quickly told Matt not to order food for them tonight, that he already had something in the oven.

He didn't, so he was quick to throw some potatoes and chicken legs into a Dutch oven with a can of cream of mushroom. An old recipe from his mom. One of the few good things she had passed onto him before he had to run. Not the best thing in the world, and it could probably use some spices, but it did the trick.

He wasn't making it out of any affection for her, or because he wanted to share her memory in any way with Matt. He was never going to see her again and he doubted she'd be thrilled if he turned up on her stoop.

Nah, it was actually just a good recipe. One of the few

good things he remembered about her before he left. He pushed the memory away. He didn't want it to ruin his night.

He decided to add a sprinkling of a few other things so it wasn't entirely hers, though. A little garlic, a little lemon. There, now it was his recipe.

Matt came back an hour later, bursting through the door with a wide smile and seeking out TJ like they were bound together with elastic bands that had been pulled tight. His large arms wrapped around TJ's middle, his nose pressing to the crook of his neck and inhaling deeply.

"Something smells good."

"That's the chicken. It should be done. I can take it out of the oven."

Matt didn't let him go. He gripped TJ tighter, which TJ wasn't opposed to, so he didn't try to get away. TJ stayed right where he was.

"No, it's you," Matt said, his voice a low rumble that went right to TJ's cock.

He shivered.

Jesus. It was one thing to love the guy, but why did he have to be so hot for him?

It was almost unfair.

Enjoy it while it lasts, hissed the little voice inside his head. *When he realizes he can find better, he won't be kissing and nosing at your neck ever again.*

He swallowed hard. Maybe his scent changed, because Matt pulled back quickly. "Are you okay?"

TJ swallowed, pulling himself out of Matt's arms for just a moment. "Yeah." He took the chicken out of the oven, turned it off, and then spun around to face him.

Matt looked a little lost, like an oversized puppy, afraid he'd done something wrong. "I won't touch you if you don't want me to."

TJ almost snorted. "That's definitely not the problem."

"Then what is?" Matt looked at the Dutch oven cooling on the stove. He glanced around the kitchen and even down at the floor, as though making sure he hadn't left a mess this morning or tracked in mud.

TJ thought about what Diane had said.

She thought they were a thing.

Not a *fling* thing.

But a *thing* thing.

Maybe even mates.

So, fuck it. TJ pushed the horrible little thoughts out of his head and moved smoothly back into Matt's arms, kissing his big square jaw. Then his mouth.

Matt seemed surprised, but he relaxed quickly, his hands resting pleasantly on TJ's waist.

TJ hummed against Matthew's mouth. The man's tongue was liquid against TJ's. He tasted a little like sugar, coffee, and chocolate.

Yes, so good. He'd said to himself he didn't want bad memories, bad thoughts, ruining his night, and he meant it.

"I need you," TJ said. He needed Matt, right now. He wished with everything inside him that they were mates. That he could have what he saw so many other shifters before him have. Charlie, Cindy, and Trisha were lab experiments like him, and they got something like this. They got the whole true love thing.

Maybe, just maybe...

Matt growled, swooping TJ into his arms with a quick motion and rushing them to the couch.

It was as good as any other place. TJ was excited. He'd ridden Matt here before. He figured that was what Matt wanted when the guy set him down on the cushions, kissing him again.

"Need you," TJ said between kisses, like a mantra, his dick swelling uncomfortably. He needed to get out of his pants. At the same time, the gentle torture was delicious.

He curled his toes and pulled at Matt's shirt.

Matt took the hint and lifted it off himself, his arms pulling upward as the shirt came off, exposing the muscles of his belly and chest. His biceps seemed to flex without intent, and his pants suddenly hung low on his hips, exposing the V shape that would lead down, down, down to what TJ really wanted.

He wet his lips, wanting Matt's penis in his mouth more than anything else.

Matt tossed his shirt away, staring at TJ on his knees above him.

"You're so fucking beautiful."

TJ resisted the urge to roll his eyes while he undid the button of Matt's pants.

"I mean it." Matt smiled, that stupid, handsome, stom-ach-fluttering smile as his big hands cupped TJ's face. "You'll believe me one day."

That made TJ pause.

One day. Like he was planning on being here, doing this with him, for a long time coming.

"Might take years for that to kick in."

Matt's eyes seemed to flash and dance, amused. "I can be patient."

Jesus Christ. Was he serious?

TJ didn't like feeling like was getting swept away like this, the heat of the moment making his thoughts all jumbled.

He wanted some of that control back, so he made sure to stare Matt in the eyes while he slowly, so slowly, pulled the metal zipper of his jeans down. The teeth of the zipper opened wide enough for TJ to stick his hand inside and grip the hot length of Matthew's cock.

Matt's dark lips parted in a near-silent gasp. He arched into TJ's touch, a heavy hand resting on his shoulder.

"Th-that's what I want." Matt shuddered, rocking into TJ's hand before he sent TJ a playful glance. "Not too much, though."

"I know." TJ wet his lips, using both hands for now. "You want to finish inside me?"

He tried to make it sound as sensual as possible, so he was only a little shocked when Matt shook his head. "No."

TJ's hands stilled, but then he grinned and sped up the motion of his hands, using some of the slick precum that formed to make it easier.

Wetter.

"In my mouth, then?" he asked, looking forward to it. He knew Matt liked it when he did that, swallowing him down and taking everything he had to give.

Still, Matt shook his head. "No, I mean, yes, I would want that, but there's something else."

TJ tried to think of anything it could be. The sex he and Matt had, while always extremely pleasurable, was, for lack of a better term, vanilla.

They did different positions, sure, but nothing outlandish. TJ was never on his head doing a half-hand-stand while Matt took him, and there was no way he wanted to do any hardcore BDSM shit.

Not his style.

If that was what Matt was into, would he let him?

Matt cupped his cheek and kissed him. "I want you to be inside me this time."

TJ barked a laugh.

Matt pulled back, his face twisting as though offended.

"I'm sorry. I'm really sorry," TJ said quickly, unable to stop from smiling. "I'm just so relieved. God, you have no idea."

"Really?" Matt didn't seem so sure. "What did you think I was going to ask you for?"

"I don't know, some *Fifty Shades* shit, I guess."

Matt kept looking at him like he had no clue what that was.

Right. Of course he didn't.

TJ explained as best he could about a set of sexy books and movies he'd never read or seen but had heard all kinds of things about.

Matt frowned harder. "I would *never* hit you."

"No, that's not... I know you wouldn't do it unless I liked it or, at the very least, agreed to let you try it."

This seemed to confuse Matt even more. "Why would you ever agree to let me hit you at all?"

This was both going badly and getting funnier by the minute.

So TJ explained again.

Matt finally seemed to understand. Sort of. And he didn't seem altogether thrilled. "Well, I wouldn't want to do that to you. Even with a *safe word*. I... don't like the idea."

TJ was relieved. He liked the sex they were having. Taking over was... a little worrisome, but he could do that.

That and hearing Matt tell him so firmly that he had no sexual interest in whips or slaps took something bulky and heavy off his shoulders.

"I don't like it either, but I don't think you minded it so much when I let you tie my hands above my head to the bed."

"I never..." Matt started then stopped, red coloring his cheeks.

TJ grinned. He wasn't entirely sure how his instincts and senses were picking all this up, but he could smell the change in Matt.

The scent of him was thicker than it had been a second ago. A heavy, spicy musk that was pleasant to TJ's nostrils wafted around him. It was the same scent Matt let off whenever they had sex.

"I... well... maybe we can think about that later."

TJ barely held back a snort. He didn't think Matt would appreciate it if he kept laughing at him.

So he put his arms around Matt's neck and kissed him instead.

Matt's eyes flew wide, but he melted into it as quickly as he always did. His hard, strong body softened around TJ. He leaned into the kiss, his hands back on TJ's hips, fingers stroking his waist in a pleasant way that made TJ shiver. Matt's tongue did that thing where it slid like liquid into his mouth, making TJ feel a little melty, too.

He was really going to do this. Matt was actually going to let him take the lead.

Even as he and Matt pulled the rest of their clothes off, getting hot and heavy on the couch, TJ still felt a twinge of nerves.

No. He could do this. Matt was good at talking to him. They had an understanding, and he'd let TJ know if there was anything he did that hurt him.

TJ kept thinking about that as he got to his knees between Matt's legs.

TJ found it easier the first few times to take Matt's big cock into himself whenever he was a little extra relaxed.

No better way to do it than like this.

Matt's mouth dropped open, his head fell back, and his

hands gripped a little too tightly in TJ's hair when TJ sucked the top of Matt's penis into his mouth.

TJ loved this. He didn't entirely appreciate the immediate taste, but it got better as he wet Matt's shaft. However, what he adored the most was the strange feeling of power that came over him whenever he did this.

It wasn't right. Made no sense. He was the one on his knees, but he felt like he was in total control as Matt gasped for breath and started to gently thrust into his mouth. He wanted more of that. He wanted to make Matt feel good, but he also wanted to make himself feel good.

With one hand, he massaged Matt's testicles, being careful as he took them into his hand. He barely did anything but let them sit in his palm and Matt shouted, reached down, and gripped the base of his dick, as though stopping himself from coming.

"Fuck," he cursed then smiled breathlessly. "You're driving me crazy."

TJ wiped his mouth with the back of his hand. "I barely touched you."

He couldn't help the amusement in his voice. Matt didn't seem to mind. There was something in Matt's eyes TJ couldn't place as he leaned in and kissed TJ again. He didn't seem to mind where TJ's mouth had just been.

He never seemed to mind.

TJ wanted to climb into his lap. He wanted to wrap his legs around Matt's strong thighs before he remembered what they were supposed to be doing.

He set next to Matt on the couch instead.

Matt looked at him curiously.

"It, uh, might be easier if you control the rhythm."

Then he would hurt less.

Matt grinned, getting to his knees and reaching under the couch cushion.

It was embarrassing how quickly they'd started hiding little bottles around the house. Bottles and small travel packs of soft wipes. Always in places where they could keep something to slick the way and clean up without needing to get up and leave their space right away.

He still felt his face going warm as he grabbed the bottle. Matt had to help him twist the cap off.

"Don't know why I'm so nervous." His hands actually shook a little.

"It's normal," Matt said, as if he had all the experience in the world with this sort of thing.

"You should be the nervous one. I'm about to take your V card."

"My... oh, right." Matt chuckled, turning the bottle over and pouring some of the slick oil onto TJ's palm. It warmed to the touch. "I am nervous."

"No, you're not."

"I am."

TJ shook his head. "You're great at hiding it."

He was. TJ couldn't tell. The guy wasn't exactly a statue, but he was doing the thing he did when he was getting hard to read. He hid his emotions incredibly well when he wanted to.

Matt shocked him when he slid two of his fingers into the lube in TJ's hand, and then reached around and...

Oh.

Holy shit.

Matt grinned at TJ, facing him, not exactly giving him a full-on show, but that somehow made it better than TJ would have thought.

"G-get yourself ready for me."

Matt nodded at TJ's cock.

Right. TJ wrapped his slick hand around his dick and coated himself. He could barely take his eyes off of Matt, though.

Matt seemed to struggle at first, his brow furrowing, but then Matt wet his lips and seemed to relax.

TJ felt an enormous amount of guilt. "Does it hurt?"

Should they move to the bed instead of on the couch? Did TJ needed to take more time to prepare him?

TJ's dick was... well, smaller than Matt's, but he didn't think it was anything to sneeze at either. It would still hurt if they didn't do this right.

"No." Matt shook his head. "I'm fine. I've been... practicing."

TJ's breath caught. His voice came out in a tiny squeak. "Practicing?"

Matt's lips quirked. He nodded. "Yes. For when we could do this."

He pulled his fingers away, using one of the moisturized wipes on his hands before lifting his leg over TJ's hips to straddle him.

TJ held so still. He could hardly move. Could hardly think about anything other than how lucky he was.

Matt kissed him softly. "I've been thinking about this for a while now."

He talked like he was the lucky one. Like TJ was the real prize here. It was so weird. Kind of scared TJ how much he liked it, too.

TJ held on to Matt's thighs, feeling hard muscle beneath soft, tanned skin. He had to say something here. "You ready?"

Matt grinned, nodding eagerly as TJ guided his cock to

Matt's tight ring of muscle, and Matt eased himself down, down, down.

The clenching heat was intense. It was unlike anything TJ had ever felt before in his life. He gritted his teeth, toes curling.

Oh fuck, no, he was going to come already, and he didn't want to. He wanted this to last. He wanted Matt to feel good.

Matt moved his hips. He must have thrust up and down three or four times at the most before TJ, to his eternal shame, came.

He bit down hard on the moan he wanted to let out.

His hands came up, smacking over his face, hiding himself.

Nowhere to hide. That was humiliating.

"I'm so sorry."

"I'm not."

TJ shook his head, but Matt was already pulling his hands away, kissing him again.

TJ hated himself. "I wanted it to be good for you. You were... I was supposed to make you..."

"You will," Matt said, making no move to get off him.

TJ forced himself to look into Matt's eyes.

He really didn't look disappointed. He didn't look irritated. He smelled happy. Content.

"We got all night."

Oh, hell yes.

17

It was difficult getting close.

Bazyli didn't have the resources he once did. He didn't have the machinery or the manpower, and he barely had the money to continue on.

It didn't matter. He didn't care anymore. Let them catch him.

He had to do this. His child was dying, and she needed the Rachel DNA.

The problem was the difficulty in getting near it.

FUC agents were not to be trifled with. They had eyes everywhere, even when they seemed mostly focused on his old home. Digging through his work. Searching through whatever was left of his labs.

The gasoline tanks would have ensured there was nothing left alive, but those bastards could be finding all sorts of items that had been spared. They would be digging for clues as to where the compound came from. Who built it. Was it left over from something Mastermind put together? Or someone else? Someone with more funding?

There were many people in the world now interested in

shifter experimentation, but Bazyli wasn't like them. He had a more important mission to accomplish. Something of more substance than a simple self-hatred for his inner animal.

Let them be distracted. He would not return to the burned-out hole in the ground. What he needed was right here.

The damn snake was living with her, however. Even if FUC was not watching this modest cabin house, the snake was there. He would be trouble.

Bazyli bristled, irrational anger thrumming through him.

Had the snake married Rachel Four? No, doubtful. It was much too soon, and Rachel Four was too reasonable to rush into that.

He'd thought she had been, anyway.

What were the snake's intentions, then?

Bazyli should kill him. The man was living with his daughter and… and…

He took a breath.

Then another.

He would kill the snake, but this anger wouldn't do.

Rachel Four wasn't really his. It was improper for him to feel this attachment. Still, though he'd had her for such a short amount of time, he couldn't deny that he'd missed her smiles when they'd lived in the ground. Her total trust in him. How she'd called him Daddy.

No. Rachel Four was nothing more than a tool for him to use. That was all, and he needed that tool, now.

So he waited and waited.

Bazyli was in his fox shape, staying out of the way, downwind, debating his options.

A knife from the kitchen?

He could steal the car and run the shake shifter over before he had a chance to release his inner cobra.

Teeth and claws were the old-fashioned way? Messy. And if he was honest, beneath him.

But he could do it. Whatever was needed, because time was running short.

Then, a strike of good luck!

"Babe, you want something from the restaurant?" The snake shifter walked out the door, one foot still in the house as he looked back, grinning.

"Yes! Fries with cheese and gravy! And a strawberry shake!"

The worthless snake grinned, nodded, and clicked his keys at the car. He unlocked it, stepped inside, and drove away.

He was leaving.

He was leaving, and he could be gone for long enough that Bazyli could…

He couldn't waste the opportunity. He rushed back to where he'd dropped his coat, pants, and shoes, a hundred or so feet away.

Each second was precious, but there was no way he was going to knock on Rachel Four's door naked.

He came back, his fingers pushed through his hair, attempting to straighten it. She would have never seen him in a state such as this before.

He knocked.

There was a small camera above the door. Whether it was connected to FUC's computers or simply a screen where only Rachel Four could see no longer mattered.

But she could see him, because he heard the sudden heavy rush of her feet, surging from within before the door flew wide.

She stood there, red hair wild around her shoulders. Eyes wide. Chest puffing with each breath.

She wasn't wearing one of the dresses she'd favored while with him. Now, a thick, brown sweater went up to her neck. Jeans that were a little too tight for his liking covered her legs. She had put on some weight, but he could see that it was for the best.

He approved of this, at least. FUC was feeding her properly. That was good.

He had to say something. "Hello, darling."

"D-daddy?"

That word, that simple, small word, gutted him.

He had not expected that.

"Daddy!"

He also had not expected her to fly into his arms or the strength of her as she held him close, crushing his chest to hers.

She hadn't had this strength before.

Warmth pooled inside him. He held her back.

Only for appearances of softness, of course.

"I missed you, Daddy."

He closed his eyes.

More unexpected pain.

"I missed you as well, sweetheart."

He pulled back. Her smile was bright. Healthy white teeth, a glow about her that had not been there in the darkness of the compound. Her once-pale skin was tanned from the sun. Her hair longer than ever.

He hadn't been the one to provide any of it.

"You look well."

Tears flooded her eyes. "You look... I'm so glad you're here."

He was not supposed to be here. Not for long.

"There's no time." He took her hands, the urgency he'd come here with crashing back into him. Time was not on his side. "Sweetheart, you must come with me. It's important. So important."

"Okay," she said, not fighting him.

Totally trusting.

Or so he thought.

"John went out to get us some food. Do you want to come in for a bit before we—"

"No, *Rachel*. No." He must be calm. He must not frighten her. "I need you with me. There's been a terrible miscalculation."

He said nothing more than that, assuming it would be enough.

She looked at him, her expression something calm and calculating. He'd never seen this on her before.

"I know I'm not your daughter."

He jerked back.

The intelligence in her eyes, the understanding and acceptance was unlike anything he'd expected of her.

She smiled softly, as though his lack of a response was reply enough. "You made me in a lab with Matthew. You wanted to experiment on us to learn more about shifting abilities, right?"

Was that what she thought?

"Do I have parents?" Her sadness caused an unpleasant clenching in his chest. "Is someone looking for me?"

This ache should not be here, this unwelcome sensation at her soft words; he shoved it away.

"No, my sweet." He spoke to her as he had those first months after she woke up in his lab. "No one is looking."

She had no parents. Unless he counted, and even then, not in the way she was hoping.

Her lips crumpled, quivered.

Had they been back at his underground lair, he would have folded her into his arms and soothed her. Pretending to sympathize with whatever thing had broken her heart back then.

The urge was still there.

A mere reflex. A product of habit.

Nothing more.

"Where did I come from?"

"From my labs," he said, honestly.

"Is Matt my brother?"

He thought of lying. He did not.

"No. He is not." More of the truth. The truth was good and proper. He'd done nothing wrong. "He was created to protect you. From the genetics of a child Mother had stolen. The son of an owl and beaver shifter. I only needed some of his DNA, but he is more of a perfect clone than you are."

And it was because of Matthew's successful cloning that Bazyli was able to get started once more on his daughter— the true Rachel—to use that same formula and know there would be success. To make a perfect clone of her, but without the aging.

So she could have the childhood that was stolen from her.

"You made him an oversized owl?"

"No, that was already in his genetics. I changed nothing in his DNA strands. I merely aged him, like I did you."

Matthew was larger. Rachel Four was small. But she had a protector now, the snake, and Matthew was nowhere to be found. He'd failed his purpose.

No matter. Rachel Four still had the chance to fulfill hers.

"Oh my God." Rachel Four pushed her fingers through her red hair. She took a deep breath.

"I never assumed you would ask me these things." He was still stunned by this turn of events. "Did someone from FUC, one of their doctors, say anything—?"

"No." She shook her head. "I mean not directly, but... I feel so stupid. After I got out, I learned about all the other people who were taken. Lab experiments. There's lots of other people like you."

"Most of them are dead now."

She cringed. "Yeah."

Silence.

He should grab her. Force her to walk with him.

She was smaller, and her red panda form would hardly be able to contend with his fox.

He did not move. He couldn't understand this in himself.

Perhaps he was that impressed. He'd underestimated her, to be sure. Part of him had also thought her to be unintelligent. Her absolute trust and love for him had been amusing. The word *daddy* had been endearing.

He'd missed it so much in his own child.

Of course. He was a fool. Why would he not be affectionate toward her?

The only one to survive. His hopes for his little girl. But too much of her genetics were different. She was not the same, not even close, but she had the blood of his little girl running through her.

That made her *his*.

He took her hands again. "You *are* my daughter," he said it with his chest.

She frowned. "But you said—"

"You are mine. *Mine*." The more he said it, the more real

it became. "I made you. You are not the original, but you are your own being still that came from me."

Yes, this was perfect. All the pieces came together with this declaration.

He stroked her cheek, just as he used to when she was still new out of the tanks. Afraid of the world, learning to speak, and frightened of the dark.

"My girl."

Her lips wobbled. She flew into his arms.

Bazyli paused. Warmth. He was so unused to this warmth. He held her. His little girl. His second daughter. Yes. This was right.

"I love you, Daddy."

He stroked her hair. "I love you, too."

Would his other girl say the same to him? When he woke her and after she had the chance to grow up?

Yes. She would. She would be just like her sister.

Whom he could not forget.

Bazyli quickly pulled away, gripping Rachel Four's shoulders.

"There is still urgent business. I need your help."

"Yeah." She nodded, rubbing the heel of her palm under her eyes, wiping away moisture. "Yeah, I can call John or Matt. Someone at FUC will—"

"No." He shook her a little. "No, they cannot be involved." Not ever. They would spare Rachel Four but kill True Rachel. Unplug her tank. Refuse her treatments.

Rachel frowned. "They can help."

"No, only you can do that. I need your blood. Your hair. Your DNA."

Now she seemed frightened, ready to pull back. "My DNA?"

"Yes." Lots of it.

But she still looked at him with such fear. As though the wrong words from him would have her spinning around, rushing inside the house, and locking the door before he could stop her. "Daddy—"

"Your sister is dying."

Her head jerked back. She blinked. "My sister?"

"Yes." She would understand. He'd thought she would not, but his good, intelligent girl understood more of the world than he thought she would. Surely she would understand this.

So he told her.

"My daughter, Rachel, died. Many years ago, with her mother. She was just a child. Just a little girl..." His voice broke even as he said it. All these years later.

He could still remember the crash. The rain. His wife in the passenger seat next to him, impaled through the windshield with a long pipe. It had gone through her belly and into the seat behind her, where Rachel had been strapped to her car seat.

Rachel had died instantly. His wife had been alive until just before the ambulance came.

Asking after Rachel, if she was all right.

Bazyli had promised her their girl was fine. To hold on. He would make everything all right.

He promised.

"If she had been... a shifter... she and her mother would have healed. It's the healing that shifters have that makes them so powerful. More than the shifting or strength. She could have survived."

Rachel stared at him. She didn't comment on the name that was the same. She seemed to be listening. "What happened?"

He shook his head. "What matters is they were taken, I

can explain the rest to you later, but I had... I had enough hair from her hair brush. I wanted to bring back your mother, but she would have wanted Rachel to survive. So I started with her."

Bazyli clenched his teeth. Years of trial and error. His youth leaving him, his family, friends, money, and lands. All pooled into his research.

"I cloned her. You. Many, many times."

"All right." To her credit, Rachel Four seemed to be processing the information quite well. "I'm a clone, and... you made more of me? And this other one is sick?" Again, Rachel Four did not ask for too many details. She did not make it about her either.

"Yes, something like that. I thought that by combining shifter DNA with hers, making yours, that I could bring her back. She could have a chance at a life."

And he wanted that more than anything.

"So why am I here?" Rachel, for the first time, sounded helpless, heartbroken.

He couldn't bear that.

"You are here because you are a miracle." He stroked her cheek, her red hair. "You were the first to live. The first of hundreds." Hundreds of prototypes, but the first of the Rachel clones. Three didn't make it before her. Nine didn't make it after her.

"How did I live?"

He understood the questions. They were directly related to her younger sister. "I changed the recipe. Used less of her DNA, more shifter. I also... aged you."

There was no better way to put it.

"Aged me?"

"I began work on your pod a little over three years ago. I determined the problem with survivability was the lack of shifter healing. Older shifters have stronger power than a fetus or infant. By forcing the aging process to progress as you are now, your healing abilities took care of any prior incident or complications."

With her, he had learned so much. He had been able to replicate the aging process with Matt, to create a protector for her and her younger sister.

Having Matt around also served to keep Rachel Four entertained as she taught her new brother how to read when Bazyli finished teaching her and had no more time for her.

Because by then, he'd gotten back to work on the thirteenth Rachel.

The real one.

"Where do we have to go? What do I have to do?"

Relief, and perhaps some semblance of fatherly affection, rushed through him.

He held out his hand for her to take, delighted when she did. "I have a small space for her. There should be everything we need to keep her pod functioning."

"Will it hurt?"

"I will do everything possible to ensure that it doesn't." He meant that as well. "But we must hurry."

"I should call John."

Bazyli gritted his teeth. "Do you have your phone with you?"

"Yes, right here."

"Call him when I get you to my new lab." He needed more time. He couldn't have that worthless snake rushing back here before he could get her to his lab. "Please, sweetheart."

Rachel Four took a deep breath and then nodded. "Okay, but I'm smaller. I can shift and climb on your back, and you can run the rest of the way there. Can I go inside and get a bag for my clothes?"

He didn't want to wait, but she was coming with him, and if he could run as a fox, having her small red panda holding tightly to the back of his neck...

"Yes, but be quick."

She smiled, rushing inside.

Bazyli watched the road. He was unsure where the local dining areas were in this town. It sounded like John was leaving to make an order. Or a pickup? Bazyli wanted to get out of there before he came back.

Luckily, Rachel Four returned quickly, a black backpack in her hands. Likely it had been provided to her by FUC. She quickly undressed, loaded her clothes inside, and strapped the bag around her chest before shifting.

She shrank down, the little red panda coming into existence.

He'd refused to let her shift and run and play as often as she liked when she had been in his care. He hadn't allowed her to leave the compound, though he knew she'd snuck off from time to time.

Now, he wished he had given her the freedom to shift and play and be her red panda self as much as she had pleased. She was actually quite adorable.

It saddened him that he'd missed this side of her.

The straps of the bag seemed to be made of some sort of elastic material. The bag remained large with her clothing inside, but the bag itself stayed snug around her chest.

"Good girl," he said, discarding his coat and pants and stuffing them into her bag. It would be far easier to run without carrying them in his mouth.

He shifted, an easy thing after so many years. Rachel

Four's small, warm body climbed up onto his back, gripping his neck, and she held on tight.

Bazyli started to run. For the first time in months, he ran with a sense of purpose. With hope.

He could save his girl.

18

It ended up being the best evening of his life.

TJ would put it right up there with the day FUC had finally figured out the formula to fix his shifter abilities.

Yeah, this was at least a close second to that.

The next time he and Matt made love, Matt was right; TJ had done better. Matt needed some time, and it was for the best that he was on top because TJ didn't think he would have the self-control to hold back.

He felt so good.

And Matt came first, riding TJ and groaning his name against TJ's lips.

There was a beauty to the heat of their bodies joined like this. TJ hadn't been aware this was missing from his life until Matt came to him. It wasn't just the sex or the heavy panting of warm breath against hot skin when they finished, either.

It was him.

God, it was him.

He was TJ's person. His one.

His mate.

Fuck.

"How do you feel?" Matt's large hands held the back of TJ's neck, soft and comforting. Like he was holding TJ close. Down to Earth.

As if TJ was the one at risk of flying away and leaving him.

"TJ?"

"Okay," he said, wetting his lips. His thighs still ached in that wonderful, trembling way that came after a good orgasm. Matt didn't seem to be in a rush to get off him, which was strange. He couldn't be comfortable sitting like that.

Fuck, a *mate* though.

He couldn't deny it anymore. Couldn't lie to himself.

It should be a good thing.

Maybe it would be.

But Matt deserves someone better, and not to be trapped with TJ.

"Matt? Could I tell you something?" His heart raced. He had to say it, though. He had to let Matt know what he was stuck with.

Matt frowned. Maybe he'd picked up on TJ's elevated heart rate. "Of course." He pulled off TJ, sitting next to him.

Trying to casually clean each other up was difficult, now that TJ had made the vibe between them so awkward, but Matt hardly took his eyes off him.

"I started to remember my life. Before the labs. When I was still human."

Matt's eyes widened. "Did you?"

TJ nodded, hating himself. "Yeah, uh, it started coming back. A few months ago. Around the time we met, actually." Just bits and pieces at first. He still didn't have it all.

But he had enough.

"Have you reached out to your family?" Matt's voice was soft, as though he had an idea where this was going.

TJ shook his head. "No, and I won't, either."

He had to tell him. Had to tell Matt what a broken fuckup he was.

Matt didn't pull away. He rested his hand on TJ's shoulder. TJ wasn't sure he wanted to be touched right now, but he didn't move away from it either.

"TJ, did someone hurt you?"

Putting it mildly.

"Yeah." His voice wobbled a little. He hated himself for that. "My mom, uh, she, uh—"

"TJ." Matt gripped his shoulder a little tighter, grabbing his attention. "Whatever it was they did to you, I won't go anywhere."

TJ rolled his eyes. "Yeah, easy for you to say right now. It would gross you out more than my face did when I was stuck in a mid-shift."

"No, it wouldn't," he said firmly, his eyes flashing with... something. "And you don't owe me a damn thing. You can tell me details when you want, and I promise I'll be quiet and listen and do whatever you want me to do when you need it, but I'm not going anywhere. Whatever this is, whatever happened to you that made you sign up for the labs, it wasn't your fault."

He talked like he knew what TJ was about to say, what horrible thing had been done to him.

Maybe he did know. Matt was smarter than he gave himself credit for. TJ might have made it obvious what happened to him already just by his tone and stuttering.

He didn't want to give details. He didn't want to ruin the night.

Because it wasn't ruined. Matt was still looking at him

like he wanted to wrap TJ in his arms and keep him safe for the rest of his life.

TJ despised that he wanted that. He didn't like feeling weak and small, but if only for just tonight, with someone he could trust...

"I know who my mother is. I know who my family is. It's not like with you and Rachel, and so many other people who don't remember them. I just... I won't ever go back is all."

Matt inched closer. "Because you were hurt?"

God, his throat felt so fucking dry. "Yeah. My mother, she, uh..." He clenched and unclenched his hands. He hadn't been furious about this in a long time. "She would let my stepdad *do* things to me."

He felt Matt tensing up beside him.

Well, good. Better he know now and decide if he wanted to bail or not before TJ became more invested in this.

"She knew it, too. She fucking knew what he was doing and she never stopped him."

"Where are they now?"

The dangerous growl in Matt's voice was unexpected. TJ was shocked to see red in the man's eyes.

"Are you mad?"

"At them? Very," Matt's words were low and dangerous. TJ shuddered at the sound, though part of him felt a swell of pride. "Where do these people live?"

TJ shook his head. "I already looked into it. My mom lives alone, she rents a room in a house somewhere. My stepdad died a few years back." He clenched and unclenched his hands. "Too many bar fights and too many years of drinking caught up with him. Died in his sleep."

Which was better than he deserved. TJ was still bitter

about that. It was almost a nice way to go, and he didn't fucking deserve it.

His mother had no one to take care of her now, but she deserved that, as far as he was concerned."I'm so sorry, TJ."

He shrugged. "It is, what it is."

It didn't feel that way sometimes. Sometimes he was still pissed off. Couldn't shake the thought that if his mom had only stood up for him, cared more for his safety than taking care of a house someone else paid for, then he wouldn't have run.

He wouldn't have let himself get suckered into a deal with a crazy scientist who wanted to experiment on someone. He wouldn't have been trapped for years with his face so monstrous people could hardly look at him.

Even when it was over and done, recovering at FUCN'A, seeing the other experiments get to go home to families that had been looking for them and loved them had been hard.

TJ had hoped, back then, that maybe his mother had been looking for him. He'd even found her on social media and gone through her page to see if she'd made any mention of him in the years. She had one post asking about his whereabouts when he'd gone missing, but everything after that had been posts and updates about the trials and tribulations of being a mother who's son had gone missing and was presumed dead.

A lot of GIFs about being the mother of an angel in Heaven. Posts saying she would give anything to have him back, and a few posts asking for money so she and his stepfather could take a few days off work in TJ's memory.

She'd barely looked for him.

So he hadn't reached out to her.

Matt shocked him just then, he leaned in and actually pressed a kiss to TJ's forehead.

TJ was shocked. He didn't move. His stomach got melty in ways he couldn't describe and his lower lip wobbled.

"I get it," Matt said. "You don't have to say anything else."

TJ swallowed around the pokey rock in his throat. "Thanks."

"What do you need?"

"I..." TJ wet his lips. "Just, can I... for a few minutes?"

He reached for the man then pulled back, feeling dumb.

Matt, once again proving how perceptive he could be, seemed to immediately get it.

He reached for TJ, folding him into his giant arms.

TJ exhaled deep. Safe and warm. Matt wasn't leaving.

God, his eyes burned.

The guy really was huge.

But it felt so good to be hugged by him. Knowing that Matt was here and he wasn't going anywhere.

"I'm sorry,"

"Don't be." Matt stroked his hair and back. It again made TJ feel both small and pitiful while also comforted at the same time.

He made no sense.

"I'm here. I love you."

TJ tensed but then almost immediately relaxed. "You do?"

Matt seemed to think about that for a moment. "How could I not love my mate?"

God, TJ really was stupid. "I guess I should've known you'd have figured it out."

"You should have." Matt sounded beyond pleased with himself. His chest puffed out a bit with pride.

"How long have you known?" TJ needed to know that much. He would feel bad if the realization only came to him recently but Matt had struggled with this for longer.

"I don't know," Matt said. "I think I started to suspect when I realized I needed to feed you all the time. Then making your bed comfortable every night."

"You sayin' that it wasn't just for you?" TJ nudged him.

Matt grinned. He was so fucking handsome, and TJ was so stupidly lucky and in love.

"Hey, do you wanna see something that will make you feel better?"

TJ frowned a little when Matt pulled back. He seemed so excited. "Yes?"

"Watch this."

Suddenly, Matt's head and neck whipped around a full 180 degrees. His head facing entirely behind him as though someone had grabbed it and twisted it against his will.

TJ shouted, throwing himself off of Matt's lap, falling onto the floor on his ass.

Matt's body trembled as he twisted his head back around, laughter in his eyes and on his lips.

"What the *fuck* was that?" TJ yelled, pointing at his face, as if that would mean anything. "What did you... How did you not die?"

"Let me help you up." Matt was still laughing at him as he reached for TJ's hands, pulling him back to his feet as if he weighed nothing at all.

TJ was still stunned stupid. "How are you not dead? What was that?"

"It's an owl thing. I learned how to do it today," he said, rolling his shoulders.

"You learned how to do that today?"

"Well, apparently I always could do it," he admitted. "But it never occurred to me to try."

Unreal.

Albert probably showed it to him.

"So, that's the trick you wanted to show me? Freak me out and make me think we needed a priest in here?"

Matt's grin showed off the whites of his teeth. "Did it take your mind off any bad thoughts you were having?"

TJ opened his mouth to argue something then shut it again.

Holy shit.

He started to laugh. "You're an asshole."

"Do you want me to do it again?"

"No!" He laughed and laughed and laughed. He couldn't stop.

He didn't deserve this guy, but he loved him. He was so, so in love.

The fact that Matt wasn't acting like it was a huge disappointment to be mated to TJ was just the cherry.

Yeah, best evening ever.

"You made that good food," Matt said, getting close. Their toes brushed together, his hands, lightly calloused, gently scraped and tingled over TJ's arms and shoulders. "I want to feed you."

TJ felt a warm blush spread across his neck and face.

God, when did he get like this? "Are you sure the feeding thing is from a mating? You might be one of those guys that just likes to watch people eat."

"You're the only one I want to feed," Matt assured him. "And only until you're not hungry anymore."

They moved back to the kitchen side of the open space. They were still naked. TJ was a little self-conscious about it. Matt hardly seemed to notice.

"It's apparently an owl thing."

"Really?"

He nodded. "It's... to prove I can provide for you. This

will do. The food you prepared looks amazing, but for some reason, it's better when I make or buy it."

TJ perked up. "Really?" He thought about that, sitting at the island. "That might work out. I don't cook too often. I mean nothing good, anyway."

"Then I will do the cooking for us," Matt said, smiling over his shoulder while he plated their meal. "You can do the dishes when I cook."

Fuck.

He should've seen that coming.

TJ couldn't bring himself to be upset for trapping himself into dishes duty. By that rule, Matt was doing them tonight.

Matt put a plate in front of him. Equal helpings, which was a little bit of a problem since Matt was taller and broader. Did he think TJ needed to eat like a horse like he did?

Whatever. TJ was just happy to spend more time with him.

The conversation turned toward Matt's chat with Albert and how he had taught Matt more about himself, like swiveling his head like that and other mating rituals owls partook in. TJ felt a stubborn rise of jealousy, but he stamped it down before Matt could notice it.

They were mates. He had nothing to worry about. It was good that he was meeting other flyers. Even better if those flyers were owls.

"We're even invited to a barbecue at their place next Friday."

"Really?" TJ almost dropped his fork on his plate. "They must mean just you."

"No, both of us," Matt said, shaking his head. "I told

Albert about you, and he seemed eager to meet you. He wants to introduce me to his wife and son."

"That's really nice. Maybe there aren't many owl shifters around."

"Not just that, but his wife can transform into an over-sized, saber-toothed beaver."

"*No.*"

Matt nodded. "Yes."

"So, also like you? I guess I can see why they want to meet you."

He wasn't sure about how many owl shifters were flying around, but it was even more rare to be an oversized anything. Miranda, the saber-toothed, carrot-cake-loving bunny shifter was the only other oversized shifter he could think of, but she wasn't around these parts full time from what he understood.

"I might also be related to them in some way. We're going to look into it, but I hope so. Albert seems like a good man, and I'm interested in meeting his family."

TJ smiled. He was glad for him.

TJ's mother might have fucked up badly, but if Matt had some distant cousins out there, people who could be there for him, then he wanted that for the guy. He deserved to have more people in the world looking out for him, more than just him and Rachel.

They were almost finished with dinner, and because Matt was determined to provide as much as he could to TJ, he was already planning what they would have for dessert.

TJ wanted to get Matt back into bed for his dessert. They'd already had a good amount of sex, but TJ was being a spoiled brat. He wanted more.

He wanted Matt inside him now. In his bed.

Their bed.

They were mates. This was their house.

The thought was a welcome one. Not remotely frightening.

They were really going to do this.

Matt's phone vibrated.

Matt barely glanced at the screen when his scent changed suddenly. He surged to his feet so quickly their plates and glasses clattered.

TJ jumped. "What's wrong?"

"I have to go."

He was already rushing for the door.

"W-wait! What are you doing?"

TJ caught him and grabbed him by the shoulder before he could rush out of the house.

Matt barely looked at him. The easy air about him was now gone, replaced with something sharp and dangerous.

"John just texted me. Rachel is gone."

"He... what? Where did she go?" She was an adult. She could go off and do whatever she wanted, but TJ knew it had to be more than that. "What did he say? I'll go with you."

"No." Matt still wouldn't look at him. He unlocked the door. "I need to fly. I have to find her. Bazyli was at the house!"

"What? Are you sure?"

"Yes! He was on their home camera! She's with him!" He opened the door. TJ shut it on him. That got Matt's attention. He stared hard at him.

TJ stared back. "I'm going with you. Don't say no to me. I'm an agent of FUC now."

"I said I need to fly."

"So let me go with you. It's getting dark out. I can use my light."

He pushed the shift forward just enough that the light

appeared, hanging off the middle of his forehead like bait attached to a fishing rod.

Matt seemed to be considering it.

"You said we're mates. That you loved me."

"That is a low blow." Matt actually looked pissed.

"I know, and I know you want me to stay because you want me to be safe or have someone here in case Rachel comes, but I want to go because we're partners now. I can help you find her like this."

Matt seemed uncertain.

"We'll leave the door unlocked in case she comes here."

They both knew she wouldn't. If TJ was left here, there wouldn't be anything he could do but sit on his ass and twiddle his thumbs.

"All right, but we need something to hold you. I don't want you to fall and hurt yourself."

TJ didn't think Matt would let him fall, but he appreciated that Matt was worried about that.

He was, too.

Jesus, he was really going to do this? He was going to fly on Matt's back?

That was wild. He never thought that would be something they'd do.

With some bungee cords he kept for his car, coupled with a few ropes he'd used for his garden, they quickly put together something that would fit around Matt's neck and chest

He shifted into his owl shape, leaving TJ to quickly fit him with the cords.

And he had to work fast.

Any other time he would have loved to slide his fingers through the soft feathers. To admire Matt's beauty and strength—and be a touch jealous of it.

It turned out that, despite his size, he was almost more feathers than he was flesh-and-blood. As TJ tightened the ropes and cords, they vanished in the depths of Matt's downy feathers. Matt ruffled them, cooing and nudging TJ, as though demanding he hurry up and mount him already.

And not in the way he'd done on the couch.

TJ took a breath.

He didn't think about it as he climbed onto Matt's back, gripping the rope tight in his hands and using his thighs to grip his back.

His mate would keep him safe, and he'd help find Rachel, wherever she was.

It occurred to him that he probably should have grabbed some clothes. At the very least some pants. It wasn't like his shifter form was useful in any situation other than lighting the way.

They were out of time. Matt spread his long wings, the wind whooshing as he flapped them hard, pulling them into the air together.

They flew off, TJ lighting the way.

19

Matt was grateful it was night. He could fly openly and not have to worry about too many people seeing him.

His vision was excellent during the night, but TJ insisted on being with him, and he couldn't say no any longer. Time was ticking, each second precious.

What could Bazyli want her for? John had said that it didn't appear there was a struggle. The camera showed she had willingly shifted and run off with him, riding his back much the same way TJ was on Matt's right now.

What did Bazyli say to her? What could he want?

TJ gripped his feathers tighter, grabbing his attention.

"We should fly by Rachel's house. If you can pick up their scent, maybe you can follow it faster than John or the other agents."

That was brilliant.

Already TJ proved it had been the right call to bring him along.

Matt screeched and angled his wings and tail feathers, turning toward Rachel and John's home. Airbound, it took no time at all to make it to her home. He didn't have to worry about long curving roads. He could cut across whole valleys and hills.

In the distance he could make out FUC vehicles, rushing in the same direction he was heading, sirens blaring.

He swooped down when the home was in sight.

With a quick glance, he spotted two brown food bags, along with a paper tray of drinks, placed nicely on the porch. As though John had put them there to open the door when Rachel didn't open it for him.

He must have called out to her and noticed immediately when she didn't answer.

He didn't see John anywhere. The man was likely out tracking Rachel's scent.

Good. That was good of him.

But now Matt was here.

He'd already known the general direction Rachel and Bazyli had run off in thanks to the video John had sent him, but now that he could fly low and pick up a scent...

There. He had it. He just had to follow it.

He didn't know where John was, and he didn't care. Matt wasn't going to pick him up. He could keep flying low until he found where Bazyli, that son of a bitch, had taken her.

"You got her scent?" TJ asked.

Matt hooted, rolling his shoulders, as if that would be answer enough.

TJ seemed to understand. He didn't say anything else.

Foxes were quick, but there was still only so much land one could cover on four paws with a little red panda riding on its back.

Why would she go with him? What was she thinking?

It didn't matter. Matt didn't care what Bazyli had said to her, how he'd tricked her. Matt only cared about getting her back alive before anything could happen.

He followed the scent, winding between the trees and branches, trying to take care with his flying, as TJ was still on him. He wished he could soar through the sky like a bullet, but it was for the best that he was forced to glide at a steady pace. If he crashed into too many branches, or even a tree, that would most certainly alert Bazyli to his coming.

Even so, taking his time like this also kept his focus on the scent. He couldn't accidentally shoot past it so he'd be forced to backtrack. Another reason why TJ had been right to bring him along. Matt was grateful to him for that.

Until he came across a stream of water. It was thicker than the other branches; it would lead into the river, but it could also go into one of the many lakes in this region.

A shot of panic.

If he brought her into a boat...

No, he had to focus. The scent would be moving along the water. It wouldn't stand still, but if it was still fresh. Perhaps he could...

He had to choose which direction to go, but what if he picked wrong?

TJ clenched his thighs around Matt's feathery body. "Bring us up higher. Maybe we can see something in the distance."

He was fucking brilliant. Matt would kiss him now if he could.

He flapped his wings harder, pulling himself higher, until he was above the trees and could see the winding of the stream.

The lake in one direction, the wider, stronger river in the other.

TJ's headlight shone brighter. He patted Matt's side. "Over there! The lake!"

Matt spun his head, eyes focusing.

Yes! TJ was right. It was so far away it looked like a small fishing boat on the water, but Matt could tell it was something bigger. A small yacht, almost.

It was their only chance. He didn't see other boats. So he had to be quick.

This time, he did fly fast.

TJ HUNG on for his life. He could tell Matt was trying to be careful, but he also didn't want to fall even by accident, especially when Matt really started flapping those enormous wings of his.

He gripped the ropes around Matt's body, but for the most part, he tried wrapping his arms and legs around Matt's bird body and just waited for his stomach to get out of his throat when Matt swooped down and came to a hard landing on the deck of the boat.

TJ slid off, his body made of jelly.

Matt immediately shifted, his hands on TJ's shoulders. "Are you okay?"

"Yeah." He wasn't. But he also wasn't going to tell Matt that. "I'm good. Just help me up."

At this point, once he was on his feet, even the deck of a small yacht on moving water felt like solid ground.

"Hold this." Matt shoved his phone into TJ's hands. "Call John or Sam or Steve or all of them. Tell them where we are."

Matt must have been holding the phone in his oversized talons. TJ had barely noticed, but he was glad one of them had thought to bring something.

"Wait, what are you doing?"

Matt was slowly opening the door to the inside of the boat. It wasn't locked, but it creaked just a little.

"Going to check it out. Call for help."

He was gone before TJ could say anything else.

He looked at the phone.

One bar. Of course.

He called John first. Hopefully the snake still had his phone on him.

He needed to do this quickly so he could back up his mate.

THE SMELL of the inside of the boat was shockingly similar to the damp scent of the compound where he used to live with Rachel. Perhaps it was due to all the water everywhere. He hated this smell, but as he descended the stairs, his excellent hearing picked up on voices.

Bazyli and Rachel.

"Will this help her?"

"Yes. It shouldn't take too much. You're doing quite well."

The stairs and general space were narrow compared to the compound. It felt almost like the walls and ceiling around him were trying to give him a big, smothering hug. On a hook on the way down, he spotted a lab coat.

He grabbed it. Smelled of Bazyli.

It was tight around his shoulders, but he put it on anyway and kept going down, down, down.

No. That smell, the damp scent he'd thought was so familiar, was not simply from the water around him.

He clenched his teeth as he made it to the belly of the boat.

It was water. But it was also other liquids. Chemicals, some boiling in their tubes, while others were open containers that released who knew what into the confined space around him.

A lab. His father was hard at work.

Matt had to bend his head down just slightly to keep from smacking his skull on the ceiling, but it was a wide open space, as though Bazyli had ripped out all the walls at some point to make this space suitable for his work.

At the far end of the room, Rachel sat in a chair. Bazyli stood over her. Something was in her arm! She was attached to one of those tanks—the very tanks that Matthew had wanted to keep her ignorant of.

"Let her go."

His father and Rachel must have been engrossed in what they were talking about, because they both jerked their attention to him.

"Matt?" Rachel asked.

The man he'd once thought of as his father hurled himself away from Rachel, instead of toward her, like Matt thought he would.

He instead spread his arms wide and took a protective stance over one of the tanks behind him.

Matt didn't understand, and he really didn't understand when Rachel stood up, showing that she was not being tied down and held there against her will.

"It's okay. He's not going to hurt anyone."

Matt didn't believe it. He kept his eyes on Bazyli but reached his hand out for his sister. "Come to me. John is looking for you."

"I can't. I need to give my DNA." She looked toward the tank. "She also needs a lot of blood."

"What?"

Matt leaned to the side, to see what it was Bazyli was working on.

The man snarled at him, fox teeth showing through his lips. "Don't come near her."

Those tanks. There were three behind him, but only one seemed to have a glowing, pink liquid inside.

He'd seen that liquid before, in some of Bazyli's other experiments. All of them failures.

"What is that?"

Bazyli produced a knife. He pointed it toward Matthew, as if he truly thought Matthew was someone dangerous to him.

"Rachel, come here."

She was still hooked into the machine. Matt could see those tubes were draining her of her blood. It was not going directly into the tank but into another machine that pumped and whirred.

"Matt..." Rachel wet her lips. "I love you. You're always going to be my brother, but I need to do this."

"What are you talking about?"

"I'm a clone," she said, so sharp and final that it froze him. She didn't seem unhappy by the declaration, however.

Matt, however, still shook his head. "No, that's not... How would..."

"Daddy is still my dad. He cloned me from his daughter, but he's trying again, with purer DNA, right?" She looked to Bazyli, as if to confirm she'd gotten her summary right.

Bazyli refused to take his eyes off Matt. "Yes."

"Purer DNA?" Matt asked, unable to ignore his curiosity.

"Yes. I was created with shifter DNA as well as a formula that resulted in rapid aging. My sister won't have that. She'll age naturally."

What the fuck?

"When are the FUC agents coming?" Bazyli asked, changing the subject.

He thought of TJ upstairs. "I don't know. They were already on their way when I flew overhead. Their flyers won't be far behind."

Which was a relief. He didn't have to do much other than keep Bazyli distracted and talking. Better the knife was pointed at Matt than at Rachel.

He looked at his sister. "I already figured we weren't really related, but you're still my sister, no matter what anyone ever says." He wished he could keep his gaze on her, instead of checking on what Bazyli was doing every other second. "You were there when I woke up. You helped teach me how to speak and read."

"I know," Rachel replied.

"You watched out for me, and I need to watch out for you," Matthew continued. "He's not going to just want a little blood, Rachel."

"I know. He needs hair and spit and some bone marrow—"

"*Bone marrow*?"

Matt was still learning the ways of the world, but he knew enough that bone marrow wasn't an easy, painless thing to get.

He heard the gurgle and bubble of the tank. He looked again, leaning to the side a little more. A soft beeping noise sounded, like a breathing machine. A red light blinked on the tank's console. There did seem to be a small child inside it. Couldn't be older than three years old, looking like it slept as it floated. But if it was a clone, there was no telling when Bazyli had created it.

"Is it alive?" Matthew asked.

"Yes, *she's* alive!" Bazyli hissed, stabbing a finger in Matt's direction. "And you are interfering."

"What else does Rachel have to give?" He didn't believe for one second that it was only those things. Regardless of how Rachel came into the world, he was here for her and not whatever the fox was working on.

"Just those," Rachel said.

Matt wouldn't look at her.

He couldn't believe that, despite everything, despite knowing how she was born, Rachel still seemed to trust the man who claimed to be their father.

Well, he really was her father, genetically. But it was clear to Matt, from the burning look in Bazyli's sunken eyes, that he cared more for what was in the tank.

"What else would she have to give?" From his peripheral vision, he could see tools. The usual setup for any of the fox's labs. Tables, an operating bed. More tanks. More notes and scribbles on white boards.

Clean tools glinted sharp and menacingly on a cold metal tray next to one of those operating tables. Dirty ones were still scattered on the floor. As though Bazyli had knocked them down there in a fit of rage some time ago and couldn't be bothered to pick them up.

"Daddy?"

"She wouldn't need it necessarily. It would be a precaution."

"What would you need to take?" Matt stepped forward, not caring for the knife in Bazyli's hand anymore.

Rachel seemed to be leaning away, as far as the tubes in her arm would allow her to get.

She would be getting weak with blood loss soon. Could she rip out those tubes and run? He didn't know. He had no idea how any of this worked.

"Bazyli," Matt said, forcing himself to be calm.

The man straightened the arm he used to point the knife.

"Take your tank and come with me. We can take it back to FUC. They have facilities there—"

"Never! They'll kill her!"

"You'll kill Rachel." He pointed at his sister, just in case there was any mistaking which Rachel he was talking about. "I know you never cared for me. I don't know why you brought me into the world, and I don't care either, but I remember you with Rachel." He softened his voice, tried to appear as though he wasn't taller and stronger than the gaunt man in front of him now.

It seemed Bazyli might have struggled to hunt and forage for food during his exile even more than Matt had.

He looked tired. He looked weak and scared.

Matt felt the sort of pity for him that came when he wanted to help another man.

"They won't hurt the girl in the tank. They can plug her into whatever you need them to. You've taken some of Rachel's blood. I'm sure she'll give more of whatever you need, but your lab isn't clean."

He knew that to be a point of pride for Bazyli. Matt hoped it would work to point it out.

It seemed to.

A little.

"I..."

"Daddy?" Rachel asked, her voice soft. Careful. "What else did you want me to give?"

He wet his lips. Long, skeletal fingers brushed across his forehead and into greasy hair. "A piece of your brain."

Rachel jerked back, pulling on the tubes in her arm.

"Just a small piece!" Bazyli yelled, agitated now. "In case of complications. I would only need to drill a small hole—"

"No, Daddy, no. I can't."

"You would wake up and nothing would be different!" he shrieked.

Matt didn't believe him. Rachel clearly didn't either.

Bazyli seemed to believe it. Or at least he'd tricked himself into believing it. The man was capable of cloning and fast-forwarding the aging process for whatever subject he threw into those tanks. Maybe on his best days, he would be able to open Rachel's skull and take a sample without it affecting her.

This was not his best day. These were not the best conditions, and the brain was too complicated for him to ever allow anyone to perform that operation on Rachel.

No matter the reason, Matt had enough.

He marched to Rachel, still very aware of Bazyli's jerky motions.

He took her by the arm and looked at the small tube attached to it.

There was a roll of gauze, so he grabbed it then pulled out the tube. Rachel hissed but, thankfully, did not cry out.

He immediately pressed the whole roll against the spot where the large needle had been.

"Hold this here."

"Rachel, do not go."

"We're leaving," Matt barked. "FUC is almost here anyway. Did you really think you'd have time? Go upstairs, Rachel. TJ is there."

Rachel hesitated. She looked at Bazyli then the tank. Her lips crumpled.

"I'm sorry, Daddy."

She rushed to the door and up the stairs, only moving a

little slow. Either because she didn't want to leave or because she was struggling with blood loss.

Either way, she made it up the stairs.

Safe.

Matt half thought Bazyli would try to follow her.

He didn't.

He stood there.

Defeated.

Matt ached for the man.

"Come with us," he said again. "You knew this would happen. That's why you came to her."

"My daughter will die."

Matt looked at the tank. He had no way of knowing what was going on in there.

Through the foggy pink liquid, the child could be dead or sleeping. The machines kept beeping, red lights around the tank flickering.

"Rachel will live. She's a clone of her, isn't she?"

"Not a perfect clone." He touched the tank. "*She* is perfect. My child in every way."

He looked at Matthew. "You were perfect, too."

Matthew stepped forward.

"Stay away from us!" Bazyli pointed his knife again, stepping in front of the tank.

Matthew looked at the machine Rachel had been hooked into. Her blood had been sucked into it. It was doing... something, though he couldn't be sure what. Purifying it? It was connected to the other tank.

"Let me help you. If that's your daughter, I want to help you."

He was part of FUC now, even if they hadn't actually wanted him. He would do this. He'd once loved this man as a father, too, after all.

"Why?" Bazyli asked. "I'm not your family. You're no child of mine. You're an experiment. An aged clone. Don't you want to know where you came from? Whose DNA I used to bring you into the world? Who your family is?"

"I don't care." He really didn't.

Either his words or tone seemed to shock Bazyli. He blinked wide, confused eyes.

"You aged me, you said. Cloned me. Whoever my family is probably doesn't know I exist, and I don't care about finding anything out about them. You're my family. You and Rachel. As fucked up as you are, *you* are my father. So let me help you."

His pulse quickened. He meant it. Fuck, he meant it.

It was a shock to realize it.

As messed up as this whole thing was, Bazyli, with his crazy scientist shit, had brought Matt into the world. He really was Matt's father.

And his dad was in pain and prepared to do something crazy. He was prepared to hurt people, even Matt, for his family.

Matt couldn't let him do it.

The boat shifted. Voices sounded from above. A few of them.

FUC agents. Members of their aerial division. Or their underwater one. He wasn't sure, but they were here, and it set Bazyli off.

"No, no, they'll destroy the tank."

"They won't." Matt was sure of it. They didn't kill innocent people. Nothing they'd done since he'd been brought in made him think they would. "I won't let them even if they tried."

The red blinking light flashed to green.

Bazyli gasped.

Matt tried to get closer, thinking he could talk sense or calm him.

Stupid.

Bazyli swiped the knife at him instead. The blade cut across his forehead, cheek, and nose.

Forehead gashes gushed like sliced pigs. His was no different, and he was immediately blinded by the rush of blood down his face.

"Wait!" He backed off, putting his hand up to fight off another attack that didn't come.

Matt could hardly get his eyes open; he could barely see through the blood.

Bazyli unplugged the tank, hoisting it into his arms.

"Stop, Father!"

The man didn't seem to hear him. That tank couldn't be light, with all that liquid inside.

Bazyli held it tightly to his chest and raced up the stairs.

20

When Rachel rushed up the tiny stairs of the boat, holding her arm, tears rushing down her face, TJ was too relieved to care about the fact that he was naked.

He rushed to her, pulling her away from that dark pit, checking behind her.

No one followed her.

"Where's Matt?"

"Trying to talk to Daddy." She sniffled. "He just wants to save his... his daughter. The real one."

There were details in there he was going to have to get later. TJ wanted to rush down there, to back Matt up, but his shifter type wouldn't be very useful, and if he went, he might surprise the both of them and interfere with whatever Matt was doing. Might cause Bazyli to lash out.

He hated himself. He wanted to go down there.

But he realized it was more important to stay here, with Rachel.

He looked at her arm while she filled him in on what happened, the both of them watching the doorway for signs of someone coming up, though they could still hear some talking down there.

TJ didn't get the chance to second-guess his decision to stay on deck when a cawing from above caught his attention.

Maybe it was the fact that he was a fish shifter, but the sudden dive of so many birds made his stomach clench. They landed on human feet as they gracefully transformed back into human shapes, little black packs attached to their bodies, the straps stretching for their new shapes.

He recognized Albert, but none of the others. "Where are Matt and Bazyli?" Albert asked, approaching them.

An agent pulled an emergency blanket from his pack, unfolding the small square into something much larger and wrapping Rachel up in it.

"Down below," TJ said. "Matt's trying to talk the fox into coming up."

Albert didn't seem to like that, but then it didn't matter, as everything went to shit.

A scream came from down below. TJ's insides turned to ice.

Matt!

Agents rushed the door. A shout of, "He's got a knife!"

Another scream and the smell of blood as Bazyli appeared, swiping a weapon at the agents who attempted to swarm him. He had something in his other arm, which he seemed to be struggling to carry as he waved the knife around with his free hand.

"Get back!" he shouted, walking toward the lifeboat. "Get back!"

"We need to save the tank," Rachel said. "There's a child inside it."

Of course there was. Why wouldn't there be?

"Daddy, they're not going to hurt you or her," Rachel said.

Her words kicked off a lot of murmuring from the agents.

"That's a child?"

"There's a kid in that?"

"Holy shit."

Bazyli wasn't hearing any of it. He was struggling with a new problem—getting into the lifeboat and operating it with the tank in one hand and the knife in the other since he refused to drop either of them.

The agents kept a wide distance now that they knew there was a hostage involved. Bazyli leaned over the console to control the boat, but he kept struggling to pull any of the levers as it remained locked to the side of the main vessel.

One of the agents tried getting close again. Bazyli shrieked at him, swiping his knife, slashing the air. "I said get back!"

That's when the tank slipped through the groove of his arm. The group watched in horror as it bounced off the side of the lifeboat and splashed into the water below.

Bazyli seemed to be frozen, helpless as he watched it.

Then he reacted, shrieking, as though ready to dive in and rescue the sinking tank. The agents took the opportunity to rush him. Two men grabbed him by his arms, trying to pull the knife back.

Rachel screamed for them to stop.

A strange instinct came over TJ, as though he was outside of himself. He just knew what he needed to do.

TJ dove into the water.

The shouting, the chaos on the boat, became a quiet muffle when he was submerged.

And then he shifted.

He let his mouth stretch, his teeth come out, his arms shrink down into fins.

Anglerfish could grow to be much larger than what most people expected. He wasn't quite a full meter long in his animal shape, but he was big enough to swim down to the bottom of the lake in quick time.

His lure lit up and he spotted the tank heading to the bottom of the lake floor. When it landed, it kicked up the sand and mud and other things, creating a cloud around it.

The tank control panel continued to blink green. He wasn't sure what that meant, but when it turned orange, he figured that was bad.

Probably had something to do with the liquid seeping out of a crack in the glass.

He swam over to it, then gently, so gently, used his long, curved teeth to scoop the tank into his mouth.

He had to stretch his lips wide, using no pressure. He didn't want to break the tank any more than it already was.

It was lighter than he'd expected—though he figured part of it was the fact that he had access to the full strength of his shifter side. He swam to the surface, fully aware there was broken glass in his mouth, and he wanted to get it out as quickly as possible. The pink liquid tasted like cough syrup. He felt bad for the poor creature forced to live in that.

He broke the surface. Everything came back into focus.

Rachel was crying. Matt was on the deck of the boat, holding her. There was blood on Matt's face. A lot of it. TJ could smell the blood from here.

He didn't see Bazyli. He didn't care. The relief of seeing Matt almost made TJ forget what he was gripping with his teeth.

Matt was alive. He was fine.

This was good. They were going to win this day.

He was also very aware of when the aerial agents noticed him. His grotesque, ugly teeth, buggy black eyes, and sharp fins were likely a shock to see in the water.

One spotted him and stopped like he'd spotted a monster. "Jesus Christ!" He put his hands over his chest, blew out a breath from his nose, and laughed. "That scared the shit out of me."

Matt growled at the agent over Rachel's head.

The agent didn't seem to notice. Neither did the other agents with him, who looked at TJ warily.

"Help him get the tank! Hurry up!" It was Albert who shouted, who didn't falter at the sight of TJ. He jumped into the water. He'd seen TJ many times before. He was used to the ugly fish shape.

That forced the agents into action, which TJ was relieved about. He wanted these gross-tasting bits of broken glass out of his mouth.

Other agents started jumping in as well, still staring at him like they feared he would bite them.

TJ held still, keeping his breathing even.

He wasn't sure what these agents would say about him after this was all over, but he'd be damned if he gave them any ammunition to use against him for gossip later. He might look like a fearsome monster, but if anyone ever accused him of being one, or behaving in a threatening or menacing manner, he'd forever know those accusations were full of shit.

They gently pulled the tank out of his teeth, and quickly fixed together multiple life jackets for the tank.

Why weren't they using the lifeboat?

What happened?

When the tank and its gross-tasting liquids were out of his mouth, Albert shocked him by getting really close.

"Open your mouth wider. I want to make sure no glass shards popped off that thing into your mouth."

Oh, good point.

TJ still wasn't expecting the guy to really get up and in there, actually using a small flashlight from his pack and practically sticking his whole head in TJ's mouth.

TJ held perfectly still for the examination. He felt sorry for Albert for having to breathe in what was probably gross fish breath, but there it was.

It was over sooner than he thought, too.

Albert put the penlight away. "All right, change back. We have a situation above, and we're calling for reinforcements."

He shifted so fast he almost forgot that he still needed to swim and breathe air with real lungs.

"What happened?" TJ said, keeping his head above the water as he swam back to the boat with Albert. "Is Matt okay?"

The agents had gently pulled the leaking tank back up and into the boat with the ladder. Albert swam to the side of it, grabbing one of the rungs, but he let TJ go first.

"He'll be fine." Albert didn't sound happy. "Bazyli is dead, though."

"What?" TJ stopped on the ladder.

"Go on up. I'll explain everything. Right now I want to get this boat back to land, find out what's going on with that tank, get Matt and Rachel some medical care, and just be done with this whole day."

TJ shook himself out of that weird shock he felt.

He moved, climbing the ladder back to the top of the boat. He still wasn't entirely used to being naked around so many people. Matt had apparently found a white coat to put on at some point, but it was soaked red.

Rachel was trying to wrap his forehead with some gauze.

TJ finally spotted the lifeboat with an agent inside. TJ couldn't see Bazyli, but he knew the guy was in there, too.

Dead. Jesus.

Matt looked a little far away as Rachel bandaged him. He blinked and looked at TJ as he approached, as though finally picking up his scent. Matt seemed to come out of a fog of sorts, clarity coming back to his eyes.

He looked at Rachel, pressing his hand to her shoulder.

She smiled weakly at him, and as if that was the signal he needed, he rushed to TJ, pulling him into his arms and holding him tight.

TJ hugged him back for all he was worth.

"I'm so sorry." He kissed Matt's jaw and neck, stroking his hair and wishing he could shelter him from all of this. This was the best he could do. "I'm so fucking sorry."

Matt buried his face in TJ's neck. He didn't say anything. He shook softly for a while, never letting him go.

21

Matt had made it upstairs just in time to see the tank falling into the lake.

Bazyli had tried to dive after it, but the FUC agents tackled him.

The knife was still in his hand. He refused to let it go.

That, his fight with the FUC agents, and the fact that the bottom of the lifeboat was likely wet and slippery all contributed to him falling hard.

On the knife.

Rachel screamed.

Matt couldn't think.

He smelled more blood, now not just his own. The FUC agents moved into action, doing everything they could to save Bazyli's life, but they couldn't pack the wound tight enough or fast enough.

He couldn't blame them; they'd tried.

He felt... He wasn't sure, but he knew he wasn't all right.

The man he'd called his father for as long as he could remember was dead. He'd died in a crazed panic, and there hadn't been a damn thing Matt could do to save him.

Then TJ was there.

Matt barely remembered Rachel, sniffling, her eyes red, trying to bandage the cut on his face, but he saw TJ, and it was like the only ray of sunshine that day came down and hit him, making his mate glow.

Matt needed him. He rushed to him and cried into his neck, hating himself for it.

TJ didn't judge him. He kissed Matt's neck and jaw, trying to avoid the blood, telling him that he loved him, that it would be all right.

In that moment, Matt didn't think it would be, but looking back, he was glad he had TJ there with him, to hold him together.

John had apparently been coordinating with Albert. He was waiting for them at a dock on the lake when they managed to get the yacht back to civilization. Matt watched as Rachel rushed into John's arms, crying her apologies.

John held her, his hand in her red hair, eyes closed, as if he'd worried his life would slip away from him after he'd just gotten it back.

Matt knew the feeling, pulling TJ closer to his side, the warmth of the man comforting him as they left the boat. He was glad John was there for his sister. So glad he'd called as quickly as he did.

It wasn't just John waiting for them. It seemed like practically all of FUC was there. Anyone within the county.

After some coordination effort by the agents, Bazyli was brought off the boat in a body bag. Matt tried to keep his throat from closing up as he watched that, but his attention was grabbed by another set of agents, led by Albert, bringing the tank to the waiting ambulance.

They'd pulled the little girl out of the cracked glass.

He heard the agents discussing her. She was alive, not moving, but at least breathing on her own.

Whatever Bazyli had wanted to do, it had worked. He hadn't needed Rachel's bone marrow or bits of her brain. The girl in the tank was going to live, it seemed. Even as the ambulance rode away with sirens blaring, he knew it in his heart of hearts she would survive. She wasn't going to die in the hospital.

He wished his father was alive to see that.

"How are you doing?"

Albert. Matt jumped slightly.

He was so wound up.

"Fine." He was practically glued to TJ's hip. "I just want to get home. What will happen to the girl? If she lives?"

"We'll see if she's a shifter to start off with. If she is, she'll need someone to care for her in our system." He rubbed his forehead. "I might know someone. I'll have to ask her, though."

"Who?"

Matt wanted to make sure that whoever it was, was good. He didn't want that little girl getting lost in the system, not after what his father went through to bring her to life.

As fucked up as his father had been, especially toward the end, Matt wanted that for him.

Albert didn't answer right away. His hands were on his hips. He was wearing some thin garb that had been stuffed into one of those packs. He looked thoughtful.

"Who?" Matt asked again.

Albert shook his head. "I need to ask before I can give you a name."

It's his wife, Beverly, a little voice in the back of Matt's mind spoke up.

Albert had a shifter family. He already had a toddler close to that little girl's age.

He wanted to ask his wife.

Matt found himself pleased by the idea.

There was so much that could get in the way of that. Maybe it was too much to hope for. Too much work to take on. So much that could happen. Would Rachel and John would want her?

Matt didn't think so. It seemed unlikely to him that Rachel would want to be close to a clone of herself—or was it someone she was a clone of?

He couldn't keep it all straight, and it didn't matter either.

He was hoping Albert and his wife would take the girl. He hoped the girl survived. He hoped she came out all right and that she could have a mother and a father and even a brother with their son.

That seemed like the best outcome. The most positive way this shitshow could be turned around.

"Thank you," Matt said. "Whoever it is, I'm sure they'll be wonderful."

Albert nodded. Then he looked at Matt.

As if there was something he wanted to say.

"Are you sure you're okay?" Matt asked.

Albert blinked owlishly. "Yes, thank you. I know today was... what it was. Maybe we'll cancel the barbecue on Friday."

"Of course. Take all the time you need." It was definitely for the best. He wasn't in the mood for a happy dinner in three days.

Albert nodded. "I'll set something up in a few weeks. I do want you to meet Beverly and my son."

"I'd like that," Matt said. Maybe by then he would know what their decision was on taking in the little girl from the tank.

For now, there was so much to do. He wanted to take care of Rachel. He wanted to get some painkillers for his face.

And he wanted to get TJ in bed. The sooner the better on that one.

Albert clapped him on the shoulder, a friendly gesture, but the mood wasn't there for any of them.

Matt and TJ were questioned for an hour, with some pencil pusher taking notes on what happened. What time he got the message from John and why they decided to rush off and search for Bazyli on their own without authorization.

"Because he was my father and my sister was in trouble," Matt said, losing his patience with the whole thing, feeling his talons coming out, feathers forming and puffing.

TJ reached down, gently taking hold of his wrist in a gentle grip. It was enough to center him. To yank him back to himself before he did something stupid—like threaten a FUC officer.

The man looked at him strangely, as though he was waiting for Matt to make a move. To make his day, so to speak.

Matt wouldn't give him the satisfaction.

By the time the questioning was done, it was dark. A medic came over and gave his wound a once-over. He didn't need stitches, thankfully. His healing was already taking effect. Faster than TJ's healing, at any rate. After the medic applied some cream that burned, he assured Matt it would likely be fully healed by tomorrow morning.

He might not even have a scar.

The beach of the lake was lit up nice and bright when they were finished. Headlights from cars and lamps cast their white light across the water and sand.

FUC agents swarmed the yacht and the lifeboat and were probably cataloging everything in Bazyli's lab. They'd be doing that for a while.

Sam and Steve were there, pointing at this and that. Listening to what the other agents who'd been on the scene had to say. Warren, a wolf shifter, was sniffing around in his wolf shape on the beach, looking for the scents of other people.

He wouldn't find anyone else. Bazyli had been alone in the end.

They were doing their jobs, but it felt so impersonal. Matt almost wanted to yell at them to have respect for the dead and get out of there.

He didn't. He turned away.

"I want to go home." He grabbed TJ's hand. "Can I go back to your house?"

TJ's smile was welcome and beautiful. "Our house, yeah."

Matt paused. "Ours?"

TJ leaned close. There was a chill in the air now. "You barely slept at your apartment. You want to officially get rid of it? Since we're mates and all. You don't have to if you don't want to!" he added quickly.

As if Matt would have any objections to it.

But the idea that TJ wanted him to be only at his house, that he was already considering it theirs... Matt's stomach clenched.

He pulled TJ around, taking his face in hand and leaning in to kiss him sweetly and deeply on the mouth.

That seemed to stun him.

"You're gorgeous," Matt said, filled with love for this man.

He was so fucking glad they'd met.

TJ did that bashful thing he always did where he blushed and glanced away. "No, I'm not."

"You are, and you're perfect. You saved that little girl."

Now TJ seemed to be fighting a smile. "The one time my animal shape would ever come in handy."

"There'll be other times, but you did it. If you hadn't insisted on coming with me, Rachel would be dead."

His father hadn't been evil. Matt would go to his death believing that, but that made it all the more frightening, though. That someone who was not evil would be capable of strapping down the girl he'd raised and putting a drill through her head.

Whatever demons Bazyli had, Matt hoped the man was resting well, not haunted by them anymore.

"I love you," Matt said.

There had been so much pain today. He wanted to be filled with love.

And hope.

To look at the brighter side, like all those posters he saw around town.

His sister was alive, the toddler in the tank was going to be treated by Diane and Nolan, TJ was at his side, and they were mated.

It would be all right.

"Can we go home?" Matt kissed him again. "I want to be with you."

More blushing. TJ nodded. "Yeah, I want that, too. Uh, you think we could catch a ride in a car out of here, though?" He laughed nervously. "As fun as it was flying with you, twice in one day might be too much."

"Absolutely."

It was the least Matt could give to his mate.

There was still so much to get done, so much healing to do, but with his family, Matt knew anything was possible.

EPILOGUE

TWO MONTHS LATER

Matt picked up on the scents from the barbecue outside the house as he and TJ approached. Beverly and Albert seemed to think it was necessary to pull out the expensive steaks whenever Matt and Rachel came to dinner, even though they'd told them they didn't always need to go to the trouble. They insisted. Determined as always to be excellent hosts.

It was strange, how kind and inviting Beverly and Albert had been to him and Rachel. Insisting that now that they'd officially adopted the little tank girl, they were all sort of family, and they wanted to ensure the baby grew up surrounded by family.

At first, Rachel had wondered if it would be weird to be around a clone version of herself, but she'd quickly taken to a "cool aunt" role in the infant's life. Matt was still getting used to it.

Also still getting used to? The motherly way Beverly treated them all.

Matt's knuckles barely rapped once on the heavy oak door before it was thrown open, and a much smaller, powerful little figure pulled him into a hug with impressive strength.

"We're so glad you could make it!" Beverly pulled back, her hands on his shoulders. Positively glowing as she looked him up and down. She wore a thick, soft sweater that folded down around her elbows and a neckline so wide it hung off one shoulder. It looked soft and comforting, which was exactly how he'd found Beverly to be.

Matt still wasn't used to this sort of affection from anyone other than Rachel—and now TJ. He wasn't used to people touching him so often, or looking at him with adoration. He wasn't sure why he allowed it with Beverly, other than she had a calming scent he found soothing, and had showed nothing but kindness toward him. Had he been alone, he might have rejected the dinner invitations and hid from that kind of attention, but Rachel loved seeing the baby and had bonded with the rest of the family, and Matt figured if she could embrace it, so could he.

"It's good to see you, too," Matt said, still feeling oddly bashful.

This would be the fourth time this month he and TJ were having dinner at her and Albert's house, but Matt had seen them more often than that for flying lessons followed by lunch at the café in town. He had to wonder why the people weren't getting sick of him.

"You, too!" Beverly beamed before focusing on her next gust. "TJ, come here. It's been so long."

TJ seemed a little more flustered than Matt was to be hugged so tightly by the smaller woman. He was always a little shy around the people who had seen him before his shifting abilities could be fixed. Back when, as TJ had described himself, he looked like the stuff of Tim Burton's nightmares.

Still, he hugged her back. "Thanks for having us."

"Anytime. Come in! Rachel and John got here early. Rachel's with the kids."

Of course she was.

Matt couldn't help but smile.

His sister had taken a liking to Beverly and Albert's son and new adopted daughter. He didn't think it was only because she and the girl were near identical clones of each other. Rachel seemed to be a natural with kids, and had even voiced possibly wanting to become a teacher.

They stepped inside and were enveloped by the pleasant smell of garlic and spices as they removed their shoes. Beverly, grinning brightly as she always seemed to be doing, bounced down the hall.

"Albert! Matt and TJ are here."

TJ slipped his hand easily into Matt's as they followed Beverly to the sitting room. Matt's heart warmed at the sight of Rachel, sitting on the rug on the floor. Soft toy blocks were scattered around for Finn to smack into each other, while the baby girl napped peacefully in her baby swing.

Hard to imagine Rachel and that little baby were almost one and the same.

Rachel immediately looked up, eyes bright, her red hair was down and pulled back with a clip and she wore a spaghetti strap dress.

"Hi Matt," she pulled herself up easily, coming forward for her hug.

He welcomed it a little easier than with Beverly, happy to see his sister in good health and spirits.

"Hey."

She grinned up at him, pulling back. "Sorry, I pulled John here a little early. I couldn't wait to see the kids."

She glanced back. Matt hadn't noticed John sitting in

one of the chairs in the corner. He stood up, stepped forward, and held out his hand for Matt while Rachel hugged TJ.

Matt took it, while both of them kept distance between their bodies. Firm handshake. Quick and over. A quick nodding of heads.

"Hey Matt."

"John."

Matt noticed how John kept that same distance from TJ when he leaned in for his handshake as well.

"Good to see you both again. Ready for Poker?" TJ almost sounded like it wasn't awkward, being around John.

The fact that John was now welcome in this house, in the same room as the kids, was a testament to the forgiveness of the family that lived here. John had somehow been involved in the kidnapping of Beverly and Finn, and Matt heard it from trustworthy sources that Albert once used his claws on John's face for the part he'd played in working with Mother.

Yet here he was, an invited guest. Matt reasoned that if they were willing to forgive him, to break bread with him in their home, then he could forgive the man for falling in love with his sister.

For taking over as Rachel's protector.

He seemed to be doing a decent enough job. So long as Rachel kept smiling, Matt decided he wouldn't actively hate the man.

The silence lasted a little too long, though. Rachel cleared her throat, taking John's arm and looping her own through it just as Beverly and Albert came back into the sitting room.

"I've got some good cheeses here to snack on until the steaks are ready." Beverly had a charcuterie board in her hand, and Albert held a tray with drinks, including a sippy cup for Finn and a bottle for Lori—the name they'd given to the little girl from the tank.

They helped themselves and sat around the room. Matt took it all in, still not used to living a life like this—with friends who were so unlike the man who'd raised him. Beverly was smiling, looking alive and vibrant as Finn toddled over to her and hung onto her legs. Albert passed John a drink cup, perhaps a little stiffly, but it was an offering nonetheless.

Rachel looked excited. Glowing. Absolutely reveling in her new life. It was a far cry from the pale, skinny thing who'd been hidden away in the ground, when they both still believed in Bazyli.

Everything had changed, and for the better. His sister was alive and safe. Happy. He and TJ lived together and were making plans for the future, for their jobs and careers.

In a way, Matt wished everything could stay like this forever. But he knew better. Things would always continue to change. It wouldn't always be as good as this. Everyone eventually had to face hard times, too, and he'd just have to be ready for it. He just hoped it would never be as bad as what they'd faced with Bazyli.

And he had to remember: now they had more friends around them to help them get through whatever they had to face.

He leaned against TJ. Grateful that during the worst time of his life, he'd found the best thing that ever happened to him.

They made polite conversation, but Matt's stomach rumbled by the time Beverly announced that it was dinner time. Albert brought in the steaks and potatoes wrapped in tinfoil and Beverly opened the oven, revealing freshly baked garlic bread with melting cheese. She cut it into pieces while Albert put steaks on their plates.

Rachel helped little Finn into his high chair and filled his plate with cut-up chicken nuggets, which seemed to delight him. Lori continued to sleep, but Albert pulled her swing into the dining room where they could keep an eye on her.

The dinner went well. The food was all excellent. A reminder that Matt should host dinner sometime, and when he did, he would have to do his best to provide something better than pizza and beer.

The conversation was good, too. They all filled each other in on the latest news in their lives. John was apparently switching departments. Now that Mother was no longer an issue and Bazyli was gone, FUC no longer needed John for insider information. They had everything they needed, but they'd extended him an olive branch: he could enroll at the Academy as a proper cadet. He'd be able to formally train and become an agent of FUC if he wanted.

He wasn't the only one. Matt, too, was to go into official training, but only after he completed his high school equivalency diploma. He had no idea how long that might take. There was so much to learn, from history to science to computers, but he found he enjoyed school, and was lucky to have the FUCN'A resources available to him for his studies.

After dinner, Beverly got up and put two pies in the oven to warm.

Finn, who ate most of his chicken and got sauce everywhere, needed some cleanup, which Rachel quickly volunteered to assist with. Luckily, the boy seemed tuckered out enough that he didn't mind getting his face wiped down by her. Her touch was gentle against his cheeks, still a little swollen with some baby fat. He smiled up at her.

She positively beamed back at him.

Matt could remember a time when Rachel had to care for him that way. She'd taught him how to speak and move, eat and dress, and even read.

She would make a good teacher when the time came.

Matt glanced at Lori, still snoozing peacefully as Beverly lifted her out of her swing. She looked like an angel—now, anyway, considering he'd seen her when she wasn't so peaceful and knew the lungs she had on her. The baby looked to be about six months old, though it was impossible to tell her exact age. There was no paperwork stating when she had been created. Though realistically, she'd been born two months ago.

Luckily, she didn't seem to be quickly aging, as Bazyli had explained to Rachel. She didn't have the same modifications as the other clones. She would have a normal childhood.

Matt was glad she would have that—with these people. An older brother who adored her. Parents who took her in as their own. And an aunty figure who would always watch out for her.

A hand clapped Matt's shoulder.

"Hey, you seem kind of far away," Albert commented.

"Sorry. I just spaced out I think." Matt rose from the table. He'd not realized he was the only one still sitting there. Even TJ had wandered off with the others to help with dessert and the babies.

"No problem. Been meaning to talk to you anyway."

Had Albert asked to speak to Matt alone?

Matt nodded. "What did you want to talk about?"

"Actually, would you come into my office?"

"Sure." Concern rushed through him, but he followed the man.

Alarm grew when Albert shut the door.

"Is this about my studies?"

"No, not at all. All that is fine."

He didn't believe it. "If there is something I can improve on, or something I've been slacking over, you would tell me, right?"

Again, Albert smiled that soft smile. "Of course. I'll let you know."

Albert's office was cozy. Each wall was hidden behind full bookshelves—appropriate for a librarian. The shelves were packed, and not with the sort of books that looked like they had been purchased for show, either. The books were stacked messily. Double rowed, and some in piles on the floor.

A black chair sat behind the modest desk, which showed a few wear marks. Stacks of shockingly messy papers were scattered across the surface. Matt couldn't imagine finding anything in that disarray, but he knew that Albert's mind just worked differently, and he could find exactly what he needed at a moment's notice.

Matt liked it. It didn't look like something he saw on TV. This place looked lived in. Loved. Cozy.

The photos on the over-stuffed bookcases were proof of that. He found himself drawn to them. Pictures of Albert with Beverly. Some without Finn, but most with him. Now, there seemed to be a few of them with Lori, too. Matt spotted a few photos of Lori by herself, and one of Lori being held by a confused-looking Finn.

"Took us a while to get that shot," Albert mused. "He was a good boy that day. Very gentle with her."

"He'll make a good big brother."

Albert smiled at him. "Yeah. He will."

It was a nice moment, but Matt wanted to know why Albert had pulled him in there. "So, what did you want to speak with me about?"

"Right, well, just all this." He waved his hand to the photos.

Matt was confused. "Your family?"

If this wasn't about work, then perhaps Albert wanted to break it to him that he needed to cut down on their flying and hunting schedule. Though Matt had started to look forward to the excursions, he could see how Albert might need to admit that a new baby and a toddler made things too difficult.

Matt had been ready to accept such a situation gracefully. Part of him couldn't believe Albert went out of his way to still have his flying lessons with Matt, considering the new addition to his family.

It wasn't just Albert taking time away from work and family for Matt, either. On the days Matt and Albert went flying, Beverly insisted on joining them for lunch afterward. He'd tried to beg out of it and allow the couple to enjoy a lunch with just the two of them, but Beverly insisted she wanted Matt there, too. Said she wanted to get to know him. She always asked how his flight went and if he caught anything, and before they left she always made sure that Albert and Matt had scheduled the next lesson.

It struck Matt as odd at times, but he chalked it up to them caring about Lori's extended family.

"Any family, I suppose," Albert scratched the back of his neck. "Are you still sure you don't want to know... who yours is?"

Matt inhaled deeply.

Truth be told, he had been thinking about it more and more as of late.

"It's not right," he said, sticking to the same script. The easy one. The right one. "Whoever these people are, they don't know me, and I'm grown now, and it's just too weird to have an adult show up on some poor couple's door and throw all this into their laps."

Albert nodded, staying quiet for a moment that felt suffocating.

Matt felt he had to fill it. "What if their son is dead? Me showing up will just open those wounds. And if he's alive, he'd be a little kid. It would be too weird to expect strangers to care about anything I'm up to. People got lives to live."

Unsaid was the fact that he wasn't sure if he could deal with the rejection. He already had to struggle with the abuse from Bazyli and the truth that he wasn't who he'd said he'd been. But to find another family, just for them to turn him away?

No, it was better to just keep the status quo. Things were good as they were.

He thought of TJ. How happy he was, late at night, warm in a real bed, spooned up behind the guy.

He thought of his sister, smiling and healthy, even if it was with John.

And these wonderful people here who befriended him. Invited him to dinner, allowed him to be part of Lori's life when he had zero right to ever look on that little girl ever again.

Matt was satisfied.

Even if there were nights he lay awake wondering if he should look into it.

Should he find out, for his own peace of mind? Knowing who they were didn't mean he had to knock on their doors.

But he thought that finding out their identities and realizing they were happy and blissfully unaware of his existence, living a life that had no place for him, would simply tear open a new wound he didn't need.

"It's up to you," Albert said, a finality in his voice. "But if you ever change your mind, say the word and... and FUC will look into it."

The way Albert said it suddenly made Matt realize: FUC already knew. Matt had given them more than enough blood and DNA to track any relatives he might have.

And as part of FUC, Albert and Beverly already knew.

He felt a little dumb not figuring it out sooner.

He couldn't hold it in. "Are they happy, at least?"

Albert startled, like he hadn't expected that question.

"Yes," he breathed. "Yes, very. That doesn't mean finding out about you would make them unhappy," he added quickly.

Albert then hesitated, one hand on his hip, the other rubbing his jaw.

"Or," Albert started carefully. "Or that, if you learn who they are, it will mean you care any less about Rachel. Or Bazyli."

Oh.

Oh, that struck him painfully in a new, rusty knife-twisting kind of way he hadn't seen coming.

Was that really what his problem was?

Did he hold back from finding his family because he didn't want to move on from Rachel?

Neither of them had a mother or father now, though technically, by genetics, Bazyli was the source of half of Rachel's DNA. That was her identity, it was where she came from. She was officially an orphan. But if Matt found his parents, would that put distance between him and Rachel?

"I'll think about it," Matt said, only because he didn't want Albert and Beverly asking about this a month from now. In reality, he wished the topic could be dropped forever.

"All right. Good." Albert grinned and patted Matt's shoulder, his hand a warm, friendly presence. Then Albert clapped him on the back, then turned towards the door, completely changing the subject. "I'm dying for that pie and ice cream. You ready for some? I might've kept you in here a little too long."

"Yes, please," Matt said, eager to change the subject.

"I'll grab the ice cream." Albert went ahead, but Matt lingered behind. Before he left the office, he glanced at the wall.

Stopped.

Just above the light switch, another hanging photo caught his attention.

He had to look closer.

He frowned.

He thought it was a bear, at first. It should be a bear.

Is that what Beverly's animal was?

He'd forgotten if he'd known what her shifter shape was, but now, looking at this photo, he suddenly recalled a conversation he'd had with Albert. One of their first, at the café... many months ago. Albert had told Matt that Beverly was an oversized saber-toothed beaver.

How had Matt forgotten that?

At the time, he'd been excited about the possibility of answers, but then so much had happened. His relationship with TJ had developed—apparently distractingly so. And then Bazyli had resurfaced. All adding up to Matt forgetting about this similarity he shared with Beverly.

And that wasn't all Albert had told Matt that day.

He'd also told him that they might be related. That much Matt hadn't forgotten, but he'd assumed that Albert never mentioning it again had meant that they'd turned up no evidence of relation. But what if it was the opposite of that? What if there was a *strong* link, and Albert hadn't said anything because he was simply respecting Matt's wishes not to know?

All of these thoughts swirled in his mind, shocking him with the realization of what it all meant.

Matt made his way to the kitchen, lost in the possibilities.

Albert wasn't looking at him, busy scooping more hefty portions of ice cream onto plates while Beverly placed slices of pie next to them.

Albert was an owl shifter.

Beverly, a beaver shifter—a huge beaver shifter... with saber teeth.

TJ, Rachel, and John were laughing at something TJ said. His angler light was out, dangling from his forehead and glowing softly. Matt vaguely heard them talking about how TJ had used it to lull Finn to sleep.

Matt chuckled at the thought, though he couldn't stop thinking of Beverly's shifter shape when everyone sat around the table to enjoy dessert.

Or afterward, when the poker cards came out.

They were playing with quarters, but that didn't mean they didn't have fun. Matt lost eight dollars. TJ lost four. Beverly won five. Albert broke even, and Rachel somehow made out with twenty dollars in profit while John lost thirteen.

Everyone seemed to enjoy themselves, and Matt would agree that it was a good night—if he'd not been so distracted by his newfound realization.

It haunted him as he felt a certainty he'd never experienced before.

But what to do with it?

He didn't know.

It wasn't a late night. They all knew Beverly and Albert would be up early with the kids so they never overstayed their welcome. Rachel and John were the first to go. As they were leaving, Rachel kissed TJ on the cheek and hugged Matt tightly.

"You're still coming over next week for another hunting and flying lesson with Albert, right?" Beverly asked Matt at the door.

Matt looked at her.

An oversized animal shifter.

Like him.

With saber teeth.

Like him.

"Yeah, of course," he said. "So long as I'm not intruding?"

"Never," Beverly said quickly, shaking her head, then looking at TJ as though remembering he was there. "I'm so sorry," she laughed. "You should come to visit if you get the chance, too. We take Matt out to lunch after his flights and I don't want to leave you out."

"No problem at all," TJ said easily. "Our working hours are different so don't feel bad. I'll definitely join you if I get the chance, though. Matt's always so happy when he comes back from Albert's flying lessons."

Albert's chest seemed to puff out a little at this compliment. "Glad to hear it's helping."

An oversized animal shifter, with saber teeth.

And her husband who was an owl shifter.

Matt was an owl shifter. The size of a small bear, with

saber teeth curving down his feathery chest from out of his beak.

"Matt?" TJ gently elbowed him, yanking Matt out of his daze.

"Sorry. Spaced out a little there."

"Are you feeling okay, Matt?" Beverly seemed worried.

"Yeah, I'm fine." Matt shrugged. "Just thinking about some stuff Albert and I talked about earlier."

Albert nodded, looking thoughtful. The couple exchanged a look that Matt took to mean *I'll tell you about it later.*

"Oh, well, just make sure you both drive home safe." Beverly stepped up for the hug she always gave Matt, holding on to him for a little too long, with one of her hands stroking the back of his neck.

Now, Matt thought he understood what the hug was conveying. The meaning that Beverly held back from saying out loud.

This time, Matt hugged her back, more tightly than he had before.

He sensed Beverly's confusion, but it was momentary. She accepted it and rested her face against the crook of his neck.

He soaked it in. Took in her calming scent, and the love that she wanted to give him.

TJ smelled confused, which was why Matt finally let her go.

He looked down at her. Really looked at her. Tried to see the similarities between them. Behind her, on the wall, was a family portrait. Finn shared traits with both of his parents and suddenly Matt couldn't *not* see those same similarities in himself.

Whoah.

Albert, as though nothing strange at all happened, stepped forward to shake his hand.

Matt shook it.

He wasn't sure who did it, but one of them pulled the other closer. Their goodbye hug included some back patting and ended quicker than his one with Beverly had, but Matt also found himself looking more closely at the man.

The subtle shape of his nose, the angle of his jaw. Things that were the same as what Matt saw in his mirror every day.

"We'll see you next week then," Albert said.

Matt wet his lips. "Yeah, next week."

They knew. *They knew.*

He was so stupid. How could he have not seen this? God, they both knew.

Did they know Matt now knew?

They were looking at him like they expected... something, but they stayed silent. He did, too. This was too big. He needed more time to process this on his own before taking the next step.

But he would take that next step, whatever that was. He might not be ready next week, or even next month, but he knew that someday, he'd be able to. They deserved it after all the patience they'd shown him.

Albert and Beverly had proven their love for him, not through flying lessons or meals, but by the fact that they hadn't pushed anything on him. That they'd respected his decision to not know. Matt felt confident that if he never faced the truth, they'd still be there for him, inviting him into their home and treating him like family.

A strange man, with the face of their toddler, but as an adult.

How long had they known?

He'd ask them someday, but for now, he wanted to mull

over this information. Wrap his head around it.

Not for the first time, Matt was aware of Albert and Beverly watching him and TJ through their window, as if they needed to be sure he and TJ got to the car and were able to safely drive away.

Like parents making sure the kids were being safe.

Holy God.

TJ drove. He reached over, grabbing Matt's hand when they were on the highway, giving it a reassuring squeeze. "What are you thinking?"

"I was thinking about..." Matt wanted to laugh. He was full of emotions. Part of him wanted to stay quiet, the other wanted to blurt everything out. "Albert asked me again if I wanted to find out who my genetic parents are."

"Oh," TJ tensed, knowing it was a sensitive subject. "What did you say?"

"I said I'd think about it, but now..." He looked at TJ.

TJ briefly took his eyes off the road to glance at him.

He doesn't know. Matt could tell. Not that he worried about TJ keeping secrets, but he could tell TJ hadn't put it together.

Neither had Matt. Despite Albert's prodding. His gentle reminders of the subject.

The never-ending invites to dinners. Lunches that Albert and Beverly insisted on paying for. Their reassurances that Matt's relatives, whoever they may be, would surely be welcoming to him.

Christ, they couldn't hint at it any harder.

The couple had been happy to know of his existence, but also patiently waiting for him to decide on his own that he finally wanted to know.

It was a weird feeling, knowing he was wanted by people other than TJ and Rachel.

He didn't know what to do with it.

"You want to know who your parents are?" Again, TJ briefly glanced at him, as though to make sure for himself.

"Yeah. I do." Matt already knew, but that was a conversation for tomorrow.

Tonight, he wanted to soak in the information.

And get TJ in bed for some lovemaking and a good cuddle.

Matt was in a mood to keep the people he loved close. To be grateful for the people he had in his life.

Starting with his mate. The man who'd brought him out of the darkness. The love—and light—of his life.

The End

FIERCE FLEDGLINGS BY MANDY ROSKO

The first three books are available in a three-book collection!

ABOUT THE AUTHOR

USA Today Bestselling Author Mandy Rosko is a videogame playing, book loving chick. She loves writing paranormal romances that range from light steamy to erotic, and has some contemporary and historical romances as well. You can find her on all sorts of platforms, including Twitch, where she does writing sprints, crafting, and video gaming!

Get all the latest news from Mandy by signing up for her newsletter: https://www.subscribepage.com/mandyrosko